Joseph's Choice—1861

OTHER AMERICAN ADVENTURES

Thomas

Thomas in Danger

Luke
1849—On the Golden Trail

Luke on the High Seas

Joseph
1861—A Rumble of War

AMERICAN ADVENTURES

Joseph's Choice—1861

BONNIE PRYOR

ILLUSTRATED BY
BERT DODSON

HarperCollins*Publishers*

Joseph's Choice—1861

www.harperchildrens.com

Library of Congress Cataloging-in-Publication Data

Pryor, Bonnie.
    Joseph's choice—1861 / Bonnie Pryor; illustrated by Bert Dodson.
        p. cm.—(American adventures)
    Sequel to: Joseph: 1861—a rumble of war.
    Summary: In the early days of the Civil War, Joseph must decide whether to defend his stepfather's abolitionist and pro-Union beliefs or side with the slave owners and Southern rights supporters in his home town of Branson Mills, Kentucky.
    ISBN 0-688-17633-X (trade)—ISBN 0-06-029226-1 (library)
    1. United States—History—Civil War, 1861–1865—Juvenile fiction. [1. United States—History—Civil War, 1861–1865—Fiction. 2. Slavery—Fiction. 3. Kentucky—Fiction.] I. Dodson, Bert, ill. II. Title. PZ7.P94965 Jos 2000
[Fic]—dc21   00-20132

1 2 3 4 5 6 7 8 9 10

First Edition

Contents

ONE

————— •◆• —————

Saboteurs!

Joseph held the lantern high, but the underground cavern was so huge that the light barely penetrated the darkness. "Look at this!" he exclaimed to his two companions.

The nearest cave wall sparkled with thousands of crystals, like a fairy-tale castle from a book Joseph's mother had read to him when he was younger. All it needed was a princess. Or an ogre, Joseph thought with a little shiver as he stared into the darkness a few feet away.

"A discovery like this could make thee famous," David said. "Thou should share this with others."

David's family were Quakers. They were hard-working people who lived simple, quiet lives.

Joseph was used to his friend's quaint speech, but it still made him smile. He knew David was right about the cave. Nevertheless, he was reluctant to share the discovery with anyone but his friends. Sheriff Underwood already knew about the big front cavern they used as a meeting place. A slave catcher had fallen to his death in a small tunnel leading off to one side. That tunnel had been sealed off. But bit by bit Joseph and his friends had discovered other passageways and explored them all. Some of the tunnels led nowhere, tapering off so narrowly that they couldn't be squeezed through. Others simply stopped at a solid wall. But this time the passageway had led to a huge room, big enough, from the look of it, to hold everyone in Branson Mills.

Zachary was squatting at the edge of an underground stream. His hand shot out, and he held up his prize to the light. "It's a lizard," he said. "Look, it doesn't have any eyes."

The boys gathered around the light. The lizard wiggled helplessly in Zachary's grip. It was a milky-white color, and as Zachary had said, the creature did not have eyes.

"There's another one!" Joseph exclaimed. "It doesn't have eyes either. I guess, living in the dark all the time, they don't need eyes."

"We'd better go," Zachary said, reluctantly releasing the lizard. Blind or not, it wriggled instinctively under a damp rock, where it remained motionless, hiding. "Pa has a big order for flour to be shipped to the army down in Tennessee. There will be trouble if I'm not there to help load the wagons."

Joseph and David stood up to leave immediately. Zachary's father owned the old mill that had given the town its name. He was a hard, cruel man. Although Zachary seldom spoke of it, he was often bruised from Mr. Young's temper.

Joseph sighed. Even here in the quiet coolness of the cave he couldn't escape the coming war between the states. There hadn't been much fighting since Fort Sumter had fallen in April, but now it was June, and both the Union and the Confederacy were training huge numbers of men. So far Kentucky had managed to stay neutral, but it was in a dangerous position between the southern states that wanted to leave the Union and the northern states determined to stop them. The tension was high as everyone waited for the fighting to start. In town, friends looked at one another with suspicion. It was too bad everyone could not be Quakers, like David's family, Joseph thought. The Quakers believed it was wrong to fight. In Branson Mills, however, some people seemed eager for the fighting to start. Most of the townsfolk took the Confederate side, but a few men and boys had gone North to join the federal army training near the nation's capital.

"I must go too," David said. "My parents have planted a very large garden this spring. They are afraid there will be food shortages this winter. It looks like I will be spending all summer weeding and hoeing."

"Mr. Byers did the same thing," Joseph said glumly. "I hate hoeing weeds."

"Do thou still not call Mr. Byers Father?" David asked.

Joseph shook his head. "My stepfather and I get along pretty well now," he said, "especially after we helped those two runaway slaves escape. But I can't make myself call him anything but Mr. Byers. Even my mother calls him that."

David chuckled. "The only time my mother does that is when she is unhappy. " 'Mr. Baker' "—he imitated her—" 'are thou going to stay in bed all day?' "

David did sound uncannily like his mother. The other two laughed; then, holding the lamp, Zachary led the way. Joseph and David followed close behind him, trying to stay in the faint circle of light. The big cavern at the front of the cave was their meeting place. They had made it cozy with crates for chairs and a table, lanterns, and even an old rag rug. The entrance was here. It opened onto a steep part of the riverbank. Joseph had discovered it a few months ago when a storm blew down a tree. The brush in front of it kept the entrance nearly invisible.

Joseph neatly stacked the lantern and ropes on a ledge by the entrance. Zachary pushed aside some of the brush, checking to see if anyone was close by. "All clear," he announced. Then he held up a hand. "Wait. There are some men working on the railroad bridge."

Joseph peered out where Zachary pointed. The town of Branson Mills was around the bend of the river and hidden by tall trees along the riverbank. Even though it was on the same side of the river, the only thing visible from where he stood was the highest church steeple.

People and wagons crossed the river on a bridge at the end of the town's main street. But far grander was the railroad bridge that was a short distance from the cave. From the bridge, the tracks followed River Street to the station at the edge of town.

Although the river was not very wide, the banks on either side were steep. Joseph could see two men underneath the trestle. "What are they doing?" he asked.

In reply Zachary put his finger to his lips and scrunched down to get a better look without being seen. "I don't know, but they are acting mighty suspicious," he whispered.

Zachary was always ready to turn things into an adventure, but in this case Joseph had to agree. The men were not working with saws and hammers, as one would expect on a wooden trestle. They kept bent over in a way that hid whatever they were doing. Every now and then one of them stood up and looked around as though to check that they had not been discovered. Neither man noticed the boys hidden in the cave entrance.

The boys stayed where they were. They didn't want to take the chance that their secret would be discovered. They watched curiously as the men climbed over the trestle and a minute later crawled out from beneath the bridge. With a last furtive look back, the men walked quickly away.

"Whew," Zachary said. "I was afraid we'd be trapped here the rest of the day."

"They left something under the bridge," Joseph observed as they stepped out into the late-afternoon sun. "It looks like a satchel of some sort."

The same thought struck all three boys at the same time. Kentucky newspapers were full of news about saboteurs on both sides. They were blowing up bridges, cutting telegraph wires, and setting up blockades on the rivers.

Zachary raced toward the bridge.

"Zachary, stop," David shouted. "It's too dangerous."

Zachary did not seem to hear David, or if he did, he chose to ignore him. Joseph ran after his friend. Joseph was smaller than Zachary, but faster. He managed to overtake Zachary before he reached the trestle. He tackled his friend, and they tumbled together on the soft riverbank. Puffing for breath, David caught up with them.

"We have to stop them," Zachary shouted, trying to pull away.

Joseph grimly held on. "If they're trying to blow up the bridge, you could get blown up too."

Zachary finally came to his senses. "What should we do, then?"

Before Joseph could answer, there was a rumble from the bridge and then a deafening roar. The ground shook, and bits of debris, rocks and pieces of wood, pelted the boys. Zachary had started to rise, but the force of the blast pushed him down again. Joseph threw his hands over his head for protection. Out of the corners of his eyes he saw David doing the same.

It was over in an instant. One minute the bridge was there. The next it was gone. It collapsed gracefully into the river. Long pieces of railroad ties stuck out of the water at crazy angles. All that remained of the trestle were a few pieces of wood floating downriver.

TWO

————◆————

A New Danger

Joseph picked himself up and brushed off his clothes, too shocked even to speak. "Did you see that?" Zachary shouted. "Did you see that?" One of the railroad ties slipped slowly under the water and disappeared.

Joseph heard someone shout, and a few minutes later he saw men running toward them. The sheriff was the first to arrive. He galloped up on his big black horse and slid out of the saddle. The horse wandered off a few steps and started munching on the new June grass while the sheriff stared at the spot where the bridge had been. "Are you boys all right?" he shouted. "What happened? Are you hurt?"

Joseph shook his head. "We're all right. There

were two men," he gasped. "They blew up the bridge. We saw them."

Zachary nodded. "We think they tied a package of explosives on the trestle."

"They were tall," Joseph said, picturing the furtive strangers in his head.

"One of them had a brown shirt, and the other wore blue," David added.

"Good work, boys," the sheriff shouted. He took a pad out of his pocket and carefully wrote down what they said.

"Probably northern saboteurs," one man remarked. "I heard they are doing everything to stop the movement of supplies. They have even set up blockades along the Ohio River."

Joseph froze. His stepfather believed that states did not have the right to secede. He had argued against the shipment of supplies to the southern forces, especially since Kentucky was supposed to be neutral. A lot of people in the state agreed with him, but unfortunately not many of them lived in Branson Mills. If the men were caught here, they would likely be hanged.

Joseph glanced at David. He could tell from David's face that his Quaker friend was wishing he had not given such a good description of the men. But Zachary was excited. "Are you going to go after them?"

"In a minute," the sheriff said. "I have to do a little investigating first." He pulled out his pocket watch and looked at it with a frown.

"There's a train due in an hour." He motioned to one of his deputies. "Tom, you go back to town. Telegraph the stationmaster at McConnelsville and make sure he holds the train." McConnelsville was a small town about twenty miles away on the other side of the river.

The young deputy ran back toward town while the rest of the waiting men milled about impatiently. The sheriff, however, would not be hurried. "I need to inspect the area for evidence," he said as he checked the ground where the trestle had fallen. He pointed to a bit of blue cloth near a fallen timber. "That look like part of the bag you saw?"

Joseph nodded. "It might be," he said.

The sheriff picked it up and sniffed. "I'd say this

has held explosives all right," he said. He pointed to two of the men. "They may try to blow up the Main Street bridge. Jim, you and Arvin go on and set up a guard. Don't want the same thing happening to it."

By this time a large crowd had gathered. Sheriff Underwood named seven or eight men. "The rest of you go on back to town," he said. "Nothing to do here."

Mr. Healey, the newspaper editor, came running up. He was an owlish-looking young man with stooped shoulders and a permanent frown. He scribbled busily in a notebook he carried. Joseph noticed that Mr. Healey had an odd-looking scar on his hand. It was shaped like a crescent moon.

Mr. Healey saw Joseph staring at the scar. "I bumped into a branding iron when I was young."

Joseph blushed. "I didn't mean to stare."

Mr. Healey shrugged. "Most people stare because I'm left-handed," he said.

"Are you going to catch those two?" he asked, turning to the sheriff.

Sheriff Underwood sounded annoyed. "I'm going to try."

"Our boys need to teach those Yankees a lesson they won't soon forget," Mr. Healey said with a scowl. Mr. Healey had come from Virginia a few months before to run the newspaper. His heated editorials against the Yankees left no doubt which side he was on.

"Now don't go jumping to conclusions. We don't know who is responsible yet," the sheriff said as he poked around the bank, looking for evidence.

"Mr. Healey's right," Zachary said. "If it's the Yankees, they need to be taught a lesson."

"The railroad has been carrying supplies to the Rebels," David said quietly.

"Even so," Zachary said hotly, "they have no right to come down here and blow up our bridges."

David and Zachary looked at Joseph as though waiting to see which side he was on. He hesitated, not sure how to answer. He could see the right on both sides. "I wonder if the Confederates are blowing up northern bridges," he said.

By now a large crowd had gathered. Merchants along the main street had locked up their stores and come to watch. Joseph spotted Mr. Johnson, still in the white apron he wore at work. Ladies with parasols to protect them from the sun gathered in groups. This was the most exciting thing that had ever happened in Branson Mills.

At last the sheriff was ready. He divided the men, sending groups of two or three in different directions. "You boys stay here," he said. "That way you'll be out of the way in case there is trouble, and I can find you if I need you."

Suddenly remembering where he'd been headed before the excitement, Zachary looked alarmed. "I have to get home," he said. "My pa will get after me if I don't show up to load those wagons."

The sheriff nodded. "Go on then. Just don't get any notions about tracking down those two men. They could be dangerous."

Zachary looked disappointed. "Tell me everything that happens," he said to his friends.

"We will," Joseph said. "I'll come by later and tell you."

With a wave Zachary trudged off toward the mill. The sheriff left with his men, and the crowd drifted slowly back to town. Joseph and David sat down on a fallen log near the tracks. They looked at the emptiness where the railroad had once crossed the river.

Joseph stretched out on a weedy patch. He picked a blade of grass and chewed on it. The sky above was a perfect blue with puffy white clouds. How peaceful it seemed, Joseph thought. If he turned his head and saw the jagged ends of the rails hanging over the river, he was reminded of the turmoil tearing the country apart. He looked back at the sky. It was hard to imagine war while looking at the sky.

"There's Hannah!" David exclaimed.

Joseph sat up and looked around. Hannah was carrying a basket of freshly washed clothes. Her house was on the other side of the river. Every day she rowed across to pick up and deliver the washing her mother did to help earn money for the family.

Joseph was relieved that everyone else had left. He liked Hannah, but he knew being seen with her gave the people in Branson Mills one more excuse to dislike his family. Hannah Douglass was black.

She and her family were the only free black people living in Branson Mills. Her father had been given his freedom for saving his master's life. Now he earned his living making wooden chairs and tables. Joseph, Zachary, and David had helped save Hannah when she'd been kidnapped by slave catchers who intended to sell her.

Joseph wished he could be like David. His friend, happy to see her, gave Hannah a friendly smile. But then David's family was not disliked—although some people made fun of their gentle ways. Hannah put down the basket and stared at the place where the bridge had been. "What happened?" she gasped. "I heard the noise in town. Did you see it?"

David quickly told her about the explosion.

"The deputy went to telegraph McConnelsville to hold the next train," Joseph added.

Hannah held up her hand for quiet and listened intently. "They didn't get through."

Joseph's eyes grew round with horror. Far off the long wail of a train whistle signaled the approach of the afternoon train.

THREE

Just in Time

"Where's your boat?" Joseph shouted.

"It's back there," Hannah cried, pointing down the river, away from town.

"We'll have to wade across," Joseph said, already scrambling down the steep bank toward the water.

Hannah followed and plunged fearlessly into the river. With a groan David followed them.

Joseph quickly took the lead as they splashed through the water. Hannah kept pace with Joseph, and David lagged a few steps behind. The muddy water hampered their movements. Joseph's shoes felt like heavy weights. He wished he had taken time to remove them. He tried not to think how unhappy his mother was going to be.

The water was getting deeper. Joseph saw the panic in Hannah's eyes as the water reached her chin. "I can't swim," she said, but she bravely pushed on.

"We're almost at the deepest part," Joseph shouted.

"Do thou need help?" David called to her.

Hannah grimly shook her head. After a few more feet the water was lower, and she flashed them a smile of relief.

Joseph listened for the train, but he could no longer hear it. His wet clothes and soggy shoes slowed him down, and it seemed as though he would never reach the other shore. But at last the water level went down and the friends stumbled onto the dry land. They quickly scrambled up the bank and onto the tracks. "Hurry," Joseph urged the others as he started running up the tracks.

Hannah reached under her skirt and stepped out of her dripping petticoat. She twisted the water from it as she ran. "Maybe they'll see us better if we wave this," she said.

There was a straight stretch of tracks before the

bridge; then the tracks curved around a hill, leaving only a narrow space beside them. Joseph looked back at the broken bridge before he rounded the bend. The engineer would need enough time to see them if he was going to stop the train. Desperately, Joseph put on a new burst of speed.

Then, around another bend, the train was suddenly bearing down on them. The engineer blew his whistle, two short blasts in warning. Joseph grabbed Hannah's petticoat and waved frantically.

The train continued toward him. "He's not stopping," Hannah cried. She and David stayed by the side of the tracks, jumping wildly up and down and waving their arms. At the last moment Joseph jumped off the tracks and stood beside them.

The train had slowed enough coming around the hills that Joseph could see the engineer's angry face. The fireman leaned out his window and shook his fist at them. "You children stay off the tracks," he yelled.

"The bridge," Joseph screamed, running alongside the train and trying to keep up. "The bridge is out."

"Stop!" David yelled.

The fireman's face blanched as he suddenly understood the danger. He shouted at the engineer. Joseph heard a terrible screech, and sparks flew from the rails as the engineer frantically tried to stop the train. The cars rocked from side to side, and Joseph felt an instant of numbing fear. What if the train derailed? They were standing so close to it that they all would be crushed. He was aware of frightened faces peering from several windows in the passenger cars. A woman screamed, her voice blending with the screech of rails. The end of the tracks was close. Too close. Joseph stopped, watching helplessly as the train continued to slide toward the river. The rails shrieked in protest. Fifty feet, forty, thirty. David's face was pale with fright. His lips moved in silent prayer. Hannah's eyes were squeezed shut; she could not bear to watch. Then miraculously, less than ten feet from the broken rails, the train ground to a halt.

Two men on horses galloped toward them across the field. The horses were lathered with sweat from being ridden hard. "Mr. Healey sent us," one of the men said. His voice shook. "We thought we would be too late to save the train."

The second man looked at the train, perched only seconds away from sure disaster. He shook his head in confusion. "Who gave the warning?" he asked. "We couldn't reach the stationmaster."

Frightened passengers emerged from the cars. They laughed and hugged one another as though they were amazed to be alive and unhurt. "These children flagged down the train and saved us all," a woman explained to the men.

The passengers descended on the three friends and showered them with thanks. The men passengers shook their hands, and the women hugged them. Joseph squirmed uncomfortably with all the attention. At the same time he felt a warm glow inside as he realized what they had done. If not for them, all these people could be dead or badly hurt.

"You children are heroes!" the engineer exclaimed.

Joseph and David blushed. Hannah grinned from ear to ear. The crowd grew as several more people, including Mr. Healey, arrived from town. They had crossed the river on the road bridge and had arrived just in time to see the rescue.

Mr. Healey took out his notepad. "Tell me exactly what happened," he said.

"We heard the train whistle—," Hannah began.

Rudely interrupting Hannah, Mr. Healey turned to Joseph. "*You* tell the story."

FOUR

Heroes

Hannah's eyes lost their sparkle, and she seemed to shrink quietly. "Hannah helped save the train too," Joseph said.

Mr. Healey gave Hannah a dismissive glance. "I don't think my readers are interested in what a black gal is doing." He chuckled unpleasantly. "They may even wonder why you two happened to be with her."

"Hannah just came by with her wash," David said.

"You don't have to explain to me," said Mr. Healey. "I just said that *some* people may find that troublesome."

A pleasant-faced older woman, one of the passengers on the train, rushed over to them. "These children are soaking wet. A wagon's been sent from town. Maybe you should talk to them later."

"Of course." Mr. Healey nodded. Without a backward glance he approached one of the passengers and started writing on his pad.

Mr. Curtis from the livery stable had hitched a team to a large wagon. The older woman made the other passengers scrunch together to make room for the children. Several of the passengers grumbled. "Couldn't she wait for the next wagon?" one of them said. "I don't fancy sharing a ride with a black girl."

"She saved your life," the woman said with a steely stare.

Still grumbling, the man moved over.

"I can wait," Hannah mumbled.

David jumped back down. "I'll wait too."

"No," the woman said firmly. "You'll all go in the first wagon." She watched as they climbed up and sat on the edge of the wagon. Then she got on beside them.

The luggage was left behind, but Mr. Curtis

promised to make a return trip for it as soon as he had delivered the passengers to the hotel in town. Except for the man who had spoken out, most of the train passengers were in a jovial mood, happy just to be alive. They didn't complain as the wagon bumped across the countryside until it reached the road. Hannah's usual smiling face looked downcast. She squeezed herself into the tiny space at the end of the wagon. David sat next to her, talking quietly.

Joseph saw two armed men on both sides of the road bridge when the wagon crossed into town. Hannah was still quiet. As soon as the wagon stopped, she jumped down and disappeared into the crowd.

A large group of people swarmed around David and Joseph and the rescued passengers. Joseph's older brother, Clay, was there. He pounded Joseph on the back. "Everyone is talking about you!" he exclaimed. "I heard all about it when I was at the drugstore getting headache powders."

Joseph had not seen his brother for several weeks. Clay stayed at Dr. Mercer's house while he was learning to be a doctor himself. "I have to get these powders to Dr. Mercer," Clay said after they had talked for a few minutes. "Tell Mother that I'll come home in a few days."

As Joseph watched his brother work his way through the crowd, he heard his name called. "Joseph!" Mr. Byers was pushing toward them. People let him through, but they frowned when they saw who it was. Many in town disliked Mr. Byers because of his outspoken views against slavery. Joseph's stepfather just ignored them. He put a hand on Joseph's shoulder. "I'm proud of you, son," he said quietly. Joseph felt warm pleasure at his stepfather's praise.

"Thank you, sir," Joseph said. "But it wasn't just us." He looked around for Hannah, but she was nowhere in sight.

"Hannah remembered she left Mrs. Wright's wash on the riverbank," David said.

"Perhaps it's just as well," said Mr. Byers. "I don't agree that black folk should be slaves, but you are asking for trouble if people think you are friends with her."

Mr. Baker came looking for David, and the story

was told once again. It was nearly dark by the time the crowd had drifted away and Joseph walked home with his stepfather.

"Did they catch those two men?" Joseph asked as they walked.

Mr. Byers shook his head. "Not yet. The sheriff has been out searching everywhere. They seem to have escaped." He gave Joseph a sideways look. "Were you hoping they would be caught?"

Joseph hung his head. "I don't know," he admitted. "When I first saw them, I thought it was awful for them to destroy the bridge. But then I thought that maybe they were northern soldiers, and I guess I wanted them to escape." He brushed his hair back with his hand. "I hope Kentucky stays neutral because I truly don't know which side to take."

"I had hoped that we would stay out of the war too," Mr. Byers said, "but I don't think that is possible."

Joseph didn't want to think about it. He wanted to enjoy being a hero. Now that it was over, he found it hard to believe.

He had to tell the whole story several times that evening. First to his mother, who looked proud even when she gasped with alarm at the dangerous parts like the bridge exploding, and then repeating it several more times for his little brother, Jared, who clapped his hands in excitement.

"Were you scared?" Jared asked.

Joseph nodded. "There wasn't time to think about it when it was happening."

Mr. Byers sat nearby in his chair, smoking his pipe. He was smiling, but Joseph could tell he wasn't listening. He seemed anxious about something. Several times he got up and checked his gold pocket watch by the clock in the parlor. Then, when it was already very late, he announced that he was going for a walk.

"It's so late," Mrs. Byers protested.

"I must attend to some business," said Mr. Byers in a voice that did not allow more questions.

Her lips pinched into a tight line, but Mrs. Byers said nothing more. From his mother's angry look Joseph guessed it was his stepfather's abolitionist work that took him out so late.

Hero or not, Joseph always had chores waiting. The next morning he milked Daisy, the cow they kept in the carriage house along the alley, and brought the milk to his mother along with four fresh eggs he'd gathered. As soon as that was done, he started hoeing the garden. Joseph sighed as he carefully chopped down the weeds between long rows of seedling carrots, beets, corn, and beans. It was a hot day, and sweat trickled down his back, making it itch.

Just after lunch Zachary came by, and Joseph repeated his story yet another time.

Zachary dug his bare feet into the dusty ground. "I wish I could have stayed," he grumbled.

"I felt bad for Hannah," Joseph said.

Zachary climbed the apple tree and hung by his knees so that his face was level with Joseph's but upside-down. "Maybe it's better that way."

It was odd talking to a face with a mouth where the eyes should be. Joseph suppressed a smile. "What do you mean?"

Zachary swung right side up, suddenly serious. "Some people don't like her family living here, being free and all. I suppose they worry about their slaves getting uppity ideas. Nothing's going to change, you know. The South will win the war. I just think she'd be smart not to draw attention to herself."

"Do you really think the South will win?" Joseph asked.

Zachary nodded. "I hear a lot of talk at the mill. Them Yankees need our cotton for their mills, but they don't understand that we need the slaves to grow that cotton. We'll be fighting for our land and the way we live. Everyone figures them Yankees will get tired and go back home. All we got to do is outlast them. I heard a fellow say some of those Yankee soldiers are already heading home. General McDowell is the one who's in charge of that big federal army that's gathering up near Washington. The newspapers say he's got twenty-two thousand men, but none of them is trained. He hasn't got time. Those Yankees signed up for only three months. That's almost over, and there hasn't even been a fight."

After Zachary left, Mrs. Byers reached in her

household money and gave Joseph two pennies. "You go to town and buy a paper. I'd like to read about my brave son."

Joseph was used to frowns and whispers behind his back when he went to town. Even the members of Mrs. Byers's Wednesday afternoon quilting club had told his mother she was no longer welcome because of her husband's abolitionist speeches. Today, however, everything seemed different. Several people smiled at Joseph as he walked down the street. "Here's our very own hero," a woman gushed. Joseph stood red-faced as she hugged him.

He swaggered a little as he walked down the street. Then he remembered that Hannah's part had been ignored, and the good feeling left him.

The newspapers had just come off the press. He bought one from the newsboy who sold them on the corner by the drugstore. The rescue was on the front page. Two Local Boys Save Train was the headline on the front page. Joseph read through the article. Hannah was not mentioned. Maybe Zachary was wrong. If people knew how brave she was, perhaps they would feel different.

"Well, well, it's the hero himself," said a mocking voice. Andrew Turner was there with several other boys from school, blocking Joseph's way.

Andrew's family owned a small plantation outside town. They grew cotton and a little tobacco. Slaves did all the work, and Andrew didn't have much to do except cause trouble. He even had a personal slave, who slept on the floor outside his bedroom door in case Andrew needed a drink of water during the night. About the only thing Andrew did by himself was attend school. Slaves were not allowed to learn how to read.

Up until the last day of school Andrew had made Joseph's life miserable. Andrew claimed that Mr. Byers's speeches made the slaves want to run off. Joseph doubted that. As far as he could see, the slaves never had a chance to listen to Mr. Byers. Why, they couldn't even go to town without written permission from Andrew's father. Still, Andrew used that as an excuse to torment Joseph. So far he had managed to avoid trouble by saying he didn't agree with his stepfather's views.

"I heard an ugly rumor," Andrew drawled lazily.

"What's that?" Joseph asked. He managed to keep his voice calm, but he looked around, searching for a way to avoid the bully. Andrew's friends circled him, blocking any chance of escape.

"It wasn't bad enough you were friends with that Quaker. Now I hear that the two of you are friends with that uppity black girl across the river. People even say that she was with you yesterday when you were doing all this hero stuff."

Joseph swallowed. "Hannah just happened by. She was delivering the wash to Mrs. Wright."

Andrew stood close to Joseph. He was tall enough that Joseph had to look up to meet his gaze. Andrew poked hard with two of his fingers on Joseph's chest.

"So let's see if I have this straight," Andrew said with a sneer. "You are not friends with her, and she didn't help save the train."

Before Joseph could answer, Andrew's friend Eban stepped forward. "Do you know what I think? I think you are one of those ab-o-litionists like your stepdaddy."

Joseph shook his head. "I'm not."

"I don't believe you," Andrew growled. His friends tightened their menacing circle around Joseph.

Mr. Abernathy stepped out of the drugstore. "What are you boys doing?" he asked. "I don't want any fighting around my store."

"We were just telling Joseph how much we admired him for saving those people on the train," Andrew lied smoothly.

Mr. Abernathy gave him an appraising stare. After a minute Andrew patted Joseph's back. "That was really great what you did," he said in a hearty voice. Under his breath he whispered, "I'll see *you* later."

FIVE

More Trouble

For the next week Joseph did not leave his house. He told himself that it was only because he was so busy with chores. That was partially true. Jared was a sickly boy who spent most of his time in bed. He had taken one of his bad spells, and Mrs. Byers spent all her time with him. Joseph's step-father went to his sash and door factory every day even though there was no business. Joseph split the kindling for the fire, kept Daisy milked, cleaned the carriage house where the cow lived, weeded the garden, and helped his mother with her chores.

David visited one morning. He perched on the fence while Joseph started hoeing the garden. "Was

Hannah unhappy that they didn't say anything about her in the paper?" Joseph asked.

David shook his head. "She reckons her family is safer if no one thinks about them. Having free black people worries some people around here."

"That's what Zachary said too," Joseph admitted.

David hesitated. "Hannah and I have not seen thee since the train. Is something wrong?"

Joseph kept working. "I've just been busy." He felt David's questioning look, but he did not look up. After a minute David left.

Joseph continued to work in the garden, hoeing the weeds between the neat rows of vegetables. It was tiring work, and he stopped to stretch his back. Abe, the dog, lay watching him from the shade of an old apple tree. Spotting him, Joseph pointed a finger at the house. "Go back to the house," he said sternly. "Go on. Go back to Jared."

Completely ignoring Joseph's grouchy voice, Abe came bounding over to him, trampling several bean plants as he rolled on his back, begging Joseph to scratch his belly.

"Now look what you've done," Joseph yelled, swatting at him.

With an injured look Abe slunk back to the house. Joseph sighed as he examined the smashed plants. He had been yelling at Abe a lot. Every time he saw the dog, Joseph felt a burning shame. Abe had been a gift from Hannah. Joseph hadn't told David that he had denied even being friends with Hannah. He wasn't sure why he'd done it. It wasn't exactly that he was afraid of Andrew. If it came to a fight, he thought he could probably make a pretty good showing as long as he had to fight only Andrew and not all his friends. But admitting that he was friendly with Hannah would have invited their scorn too.

Joseph admired his stepfather. Mr. Byers burned with a hatred of slavery and a desire to stop it no matter what the danger. Still, even Mr. Byers did not think Joseph should be friendly with Hannah. Although she hadn't said anything, Joseph thought his mother agreed. Mrs. Byers would have liked the whole issue to disappear. She had helped Mr. Byers arrange the escape of the two slaves a few months before, but Joseph knew she did not completely believe in her husband's cause. As for himself, Joseph knew he no longer believed that slavery was right. He would never keep slaves when he was grown, but that didn't help him decide what to do about Hannah now.

Joseph went back to his hoeing. Hoeing was good work when you didn't want to think. All you had to do was aim the hoe and chop. Joseph worked his way down another row. He was concentrating on his task so hard that he didn't see his mother until he reached the end. She was standing at the edge of the garden, watching him.

"My goodness," she said, "I almost feel sorry for the weeds."

Joseph leaned on the hoe to catch his breath.

"You haven't left the house in more than a week," said Mrs. Byers. "Why don't you take the afternoon off?"

Joseph shook his head. "I need to finish this. And the carriage house roof needs fixing."

His mother reached for the hoe. "It will still be here tomorrow. Go on. Maybe you could come back with a smile? I haven't seen one for a while."

He protested a little more, but his mother remained firm. So right after lunch Joseph walked to the river. It was a hot day, and he thought of the cool dark cave. When he got closer, however, he saw Andrew's horse tied to a nearby tree. Andrew and his personal slave, a boy named Ham, were poking about the remains of the railroad bridge. Hidden by some trees, Joseph watched them for a few minutes. They were laughing and joking with each other. Away from everyone else it almost looked as if Andrew and Ham were friends.

Joseph backed away and slipped past them without being seen. The train station was at the edge of town. He spent some time there watching workers loading the cars with goods. The bridge was gone, but there was still a busy section of track between Branson Mills and the Tennessee border, only a short distance away. Joseph saw boxes of uniforms and rolls of tent cloth being loaded in one car and sacks of flower and barrels of molasses in another.

Joseph walked along the wooden sidewalk past the shops and buildings on the main street. He looked in the window of Mr. Lippit's bookstore, but he did not go in. Several horses were tied to rails outside the stores, and shoppers bustled in and out.

Across the street Joseph saw Mr. Healey hand

the newsboy a stack of papers to sell. Close to the end of the street was the livery stable with a small corral outside for the horses. Beside it was a furniture factory. Mr. Byers's sash and door factory was across the alley. He was curious about what his stepfather was doing. Since he started giving all his speeches against slavery and against states' being allowed to leave the Union, most people in town were so angry that they stopped ordering doors and windows from his factory. Yet Mr. Byers continued to go to work every day.

The door was unlocked. That usually meant his stepfather was there. But when Joseph opened the door, he saw that it was dark inside. Stacks of unneeded lumber, paint, and tools were piled neatly against the walls. A few weeks ago the factory had been a busy place with the noisy, cheerful sound of hammers and saws, wagons coming and going, and, above all, the satisfying smell of sawdust. Now the workers were gone, and the building seemed gloomy and deserted.

Puzzled not to find his stepfather, Joseph turned to go. Then he noticed a streak of light under a door.

He walked across the large workroom and peeked into a small office in the back. He found his stepfather there, so busy running a small printing press that at first he didn't even notice Joseph. Mr. Byers's clothes were covered in printer's ink, and there were stacks of already finished flyers everywhere.

"Oh, Joseph, you startled me," said Mr. Byers.

"I'm sorry," Joseph said, looking around curiously. "I just stopped to say hello."

"How nice," Mr. Byers said. He wiped his face on his sleeve, leaving a smear of ink.

Almost without thinking, Joseph offered to help.

"I *could* use some help," Mr. Byers admitted with a tired smile. He set Joseph to work folding the antislavery pamphlets he'd been working on.

"Where did you get the printing press?" Joseph asked.

Mr. Byers hesitated. "Some friends brought it a few nights ago," he answered at last. "No one must know it is here. In some places men have broken in and smashed printing presses when they learned they were being used for abolitionist literature."

Joseph nodded. Even though a printing press

was an unusual thing to have in a sash and door factory, he thought that there was little chance of its being discovered. There had not been a customer in the shop in more than a month.

Joseph looked around the deserted factory while he worked. "Maybe if you quit giving speeches, the customers would come back," he said hopefully.

Mr. Byers looked at him. "Would you have me stop fighting for something I know is right?" he asked.

"I just meant for a while," Joseph mumbled. "Just until things settle down."

Mr. Byers sighed and patted his stepson's back. "I don't think things are going to get better," he said. "I'm not sure there would be any business even if I didn't talk about slavery," he added when Joseph didn't answer. "With the country divided and war on everyone's mind, no one wants to build a new house. Everyone expects to be invaded. People are arguing about which army it will be."

"Who do you think it will be?" Joseph asked.

Mr. Byers took a pen and drew a rough map. "Here is Washington, the country's capital. See how close it is to Richmond, the new capital of the Confederates. I expect there will be a lot of fighting here," he said, drawing a line through Virginia. "Each side will want to destroy the other's capital. Matter of fact, I think there will be some fighting here." He pointed to a spot on his line not far south of Washington. "Manassas Junction is an important railroad center. But that leaves all this area to the west. There is another Union army just a little to the north in Illinois and the Confederate army forming in Tennessee. And here is Kentucky, right in the middle. It is anyone's guess who will invade first."

SIX

A Sneak Attack

It was late afternoon when Joseph stepped back out onto the deserted streets of Branson Mills. Mr. Byers had sent him home for supper, promising to follow in a few minutes. The shopkeepers had already closed up and headed home for their evening meals; long shadows grew between the handsome brick buildings and wooden storefronts. Joseph felt uneasy, though he couldn't have explained why. When a cool breeze tumbled a piece of paper across the street, he jumped nervously.

Joseph glanced at the dark shopwindows and imagined unfriendly eyes staring out from each one. He thought of turning back and waiting for his stepfather, but after a moment, feeling foolish, he stepped out to the street and headed home.

A wagon rumbled down another street, and a dog barked. The familiar sounds made him relax, and he even managed to whistle that new song "Dixie" everyone was singing.

Someone had hung a banner asking people to come to a fund-raising rally to buy equipment for the Confederates. The sign promised music and entertainment, including Professor McCay, master of sleight of hand. A magician! Joseph would have loved to see that. But Mr. Byers would never approve of his attending anything to help the Confederates. As he passed by the banner, he heard a muffled thump. The whistle died away, and Joseph stopped. He listened fearfully as he peered into the shadowy alley. It was so full of boxes, crates, and barrels that there was scarcely room to walk, but he knew that sometimes homeless men or a man who had stayed too long at the tavern found temporary refuge in one of the crates.

A mangy-looking yellow cat hopped up onto a barrel. It stared at Joseph through slitted eyes, but when it opened its mouth, its meow was thin and sweet. Joseph chuckled. "You are going to have to sound meaner than that if some old dog finds you." He rummaged in his pockets for something to feed it but came up empty. Then there was another sound, farther back in the darkness. The cat arched up, and its hair bristled. Joseph decided he really did not want to know what it was. He walked away briskly.

He had only gone a few steps when he heard muffled laughter. He thought it came from the alley he had just passed. Whoever it was remained hidden. Joseph whirled around, but the street still seemed deserted. It was quiet now, almost too quiet.

The hairs on the back of his neck prickled with fear. He tried to shake it off and took another few steps. There. He heard it again: muffled laughter. It was from the alley. Someone was hiding there, waiting for him. He hesitated, wondering what to do. Should he run? Perhaps that was just what they were hoping he'd do so they could laugh at how he'd run away for no reason.

He had reached the livery stable corral when

something thumped in the middle of his back hard enough to knock him nearly off his feet. He lurched forward, trying to regain his balance, but he was struck again and again.

An egg struck his cheek, and Joseph nearly gagged. It was so rotten that his stomach lurched. The barrage continued as he scrambled to reach the stable. Something that smelled like horse manure hit the back of his neck, but at last his attackers seemed to have run out of ammunition. As he slipped around the corner of the livery stable, Joseph saw a pile of potatoes, eggs, and other half-rotten vegetables behind him on the sidewalk.

"That's what we do to traitors," taunted an unseen person. "Why don't you get some of your Yankee friends to help you?"

Joseph recognized the voice. "Is that you, Andrew?" he asked defiantly.

More laughter greeted his question. Then suddenly the laughter was silenced as Mr. Curtis stepped out of the stable. "What's going on here?" he shouted.

Joseph heard footsteps pounding away through

the alley. Mr. Curtis started after them, but after a few steps he gave up and turned back to Joseph, still standing miserably, surrounded by a small pile of rotten food. He gave Joseph a sympathetic look. "Come on in the stable. You can get some water and clean yourself up a bit."

Joseph followed Mr. Curtis into the stable. Mr. Curtis handed him a bucket. "Are you all right?" he asked kindly.

Joseph nodded silently, embarrassed that Mr. Curtis saw him this way. He pumped out some water in the bucket. With his hands he cupped water and splashed it on his face.

Mr. Curtis handed Joseph a rag. "Better wash your hair before that dries." He measured out a scoop of oats for each of the horses as Joseph scrubbed. The four horses inside the barn whinnied and stomped in their stalls, waiting to be fed.

"Is this because of your stepdaddy?" Mr. Curtis asked.

Joseph nodded. "I think Andrew Turner was one of them. He called me a traitor. I'm not," Joseph said bitterly. "I love Kentucky."

"There's rumors around town that your pa helped them two slave girls escape awhile back," Mr. Curtis remarked. He gave Joseph a shrewd look. "Maybe you helped too." He held up a hand. "I don't want to know one way or the other. I'm just telling you that people like the Turners aren't going to be fond of anyone who talks about freeing slaves. They couldn't run that plantation of theirs without them. Even your own father had slaves, if I remember correctly."

Joseph nodded. "He did. But they ran off when he died."

"Seems as though your stepdaddy has brought you around to his way of thinking," Mr. Curtis said.

Joseph didn't answer. He carried the bucket of dirty water to the door and dumped it. He looked up and down the street, but there was no sign of his attackers. "I'd better go," he said. "Mama will be worried."

"Joseph," Mr. Curtis said.

Joseph waited, but Mr. Curtis shook his head. "Be careful."

"Thanks, Mr. Curtis," Joseph said. He walked

quickly down the street toward home. At the end of the block he looked back. Mr. Curtis was still standing at the door, watching. Joseph raised his hand in a wave, but Mr. Curtis did not wave back. Joseph tried to shake off an uneasy feeling that Mr. Curtis had been about to warn him of something. At the edge of town Joseph picked up his pace until he was actually running. By the time he reached his home, he was panting.

SEVEN

---·---

Zachary's News

The Byers family lived in a large brick house on a shady street. Joseph forced himself to slow down and catch his breath before he opened the door. He had already decided he would not tell his mother. She would be upset, and she had enough to worry about since his little brother, Jared, was so sick. Dr. Mercer had already been to the house twice that week.

The good smell of fried ham greeted him as he walked in the door. Mrs. Byers looked up from the stove and smiled. "There you are. I was beginning to worry. Mr. Byers is not home either."

"I helped him this afternoon. He said he'll be along soon," Joseph answered.

A small frown passed over his mother's face.

Joseph knew his stepfather's abolitionist work was even harder on her. She had stopped attending church because the other women there turned their backs and would not speak to her.

"Mr. Byers thinks Kentucky might get invaded," Joseph said.

"I don't know why everyone is so anxious to go to war," Mrs. Byers said. Two worry lines creased her forehead, and there were dark shadows under her eyes. "Even Mr. Lincoln hasn't gone so far as to say the slaves should be freed. They should just let the states that want slavery secede."

Jared was sitting on the floor, quietly playing with a wagon and horses that Joseph had carved for him. His little face was pinched and pale, but Joseph was happy to see him up.

"Play with me," Jared begged.

"I will later," Joseph promised. "Just as soon as I do the milking and take Abe for a walk."

At the sound of his name, Abe scrambled up from his place on the rag rug next to Jared. He bumped into the marble-topped end table, nearly knocking over a vase.

Mrs. Byers shook her head. "If that dog doesn't stop growing soon, he will have to stay outside."

Abe was a big dog, but he had not lost his puppy exuberance. Mrs. Byers had removed most of the vases and picture frames to save them from Abe's wagging tail. Joseph knew she would never really banish him outside because he brought Jared so much happiness. Even though Hannah had given Abe to Joseph, the dog had appointed himself Jared's guardian and hardly ever left his side. Joseph didn't mind. He figured Jared had little enough pleasure in life, and it was obvious that he loved the puppy as much as Abe loved him.

Mrs. Byers wrinkled her nose. "What is that smell?"

"I fell," Joseph lied. "There was some garbage in the street."

His mother gave him a suspicious look, but Joseph grinned and shrugged. "I guess I'm getting clumsy."

"Change your clothes," his mother said crossly. "You must take better care of your things. With business so poor there is no money for material. The dry goods store is nearly empty, at any rate. All the cloth is needed for uniforms for the soldiers."

Joseph quickly changed. He left the smelly clothes on the porch and went out to give Daisy her evening milking. With Daisy's milk, and eggs from the new chickens penned along the back alley, plus vegetables from the garden, they should not go hungry no matter what happened.

Mr. Byers had still not returned when Joseph carried in the bucketful of frothy white milk.

His mother set out their dinner. Usually Mrs. Byers sang as she worked. Tonight, however, she was silent, and her lips were pressed in a tight line. Several times while they ate, she got up to look out the window.

Just as Joseph mopped up the last bit of ham juice with a piece of crusty bread, there was a soft knock at the front door. Mrs. Byers jumped up with a startled expression.

"Who could that be?" she exclaimed. She held down the wide hoop under her skirts as she squeezed through the dining-room door. Her face appeared fearful as she looked out the window, trying to see the person on the porch steps. She smiled with relief. "It's your friend Zachary."

"I'm sorry to bother you, Mrs. Byers," Zachary

said. "I see you are eating supper, but I need to talk with Joseph. It's important."

Joseph followed Zachary out to the porch. "I came to warn you," Zachary said. "This afternoon I delivered a load of flour. When I came back, one of my father's slaves mentioned that some men from town had come to see my father. He couldn't hear what they were saying, but they did mention your stepdaddy."

"Who were they?" Joseph asked.

Zachary shrugged. "Jefferson was afraid to say any more."

Joseph nodded. Zachary's father was often drunk and was known to beat his two slaves.

"Do you think they mean to do something tonight?" Joseph asked, suddenly worried. "My stepfather is still at the factory. As a matter of fact, he might be walking home right now."

Zachary shook his head. "I don't reckon anything will happen tonight. Pa had been drinking some. He went to bed right after supper." Zachary walked down the porch steps and turned back. "I've got some other news. You are probably not going to like this, but I joined up with the Confederate army. I'm leaving tomorrow. Since Kentucky declared itself neutral, I have to take the train down to Tennessee."

Joseph's jaw dropped open, and he stared at his friend in speechless horror.

Zachary grinned. "Better close your mouth before you swallow a fly."

"You can't join the army," Joseph cried. "You're only twelve."

"You have to be eighteen to be a soldier, although there are lots younger signing up. There was a fellow there that told me a story about one boy. He said this boy wrote 'eighteen' on a piece of paper and put it in his shoe so he could say he was over eighteen without lying." Zachary chuckled. "Over eighteen. Get it?"

Joseph smiled in spite of himself. "I get it. But surely they didn't think you were eighteen."

"They wouldn't let me be a soldier. I'm going to be a drummer boy," Zachary said proudly. "The drumbeat tells the soldiers what to do when they are fighting."

Everyone Joseph knew seemed to find the idea of war exciting. Even Clay could hardly wait for the fighting to start so he could do some real "doctoring." Zachary had dreams of coming home a hero and scoffed at the idea of danger. No matter how long Joseph talked, he could not change Zachary's mind. "It's a matter of honor," Zachary had repeated several times. "We can't let the Yankees tell us how to run our lives."

"There are a lot more Yankees than there are of us," Joseph reminded him. "And they have most of the factories."

Zachary shrugged. "There were a lot more British back in '76. And they were a lot stronger than we were. We beat them, though, now didn't we?"

Joseph wasn't sure if Zachary really believed everything he was saying or if he was just repeating the arguments heard on every street corner. He sighed. "I thought after helping those two girls get away, you were against slavery. Now you'll be fighting for it."

Zachary looked at him. "I guess you've won me over some," he admitted. "I'm not fighting to keep slavery, but I am fighting for the right to choose for myself. My pa says most of those abolitionists like your stepdaddy want to free the slaves, but they don't really want them living up North, taking all the jobs from poor white folk. They're thinking up some plan to send them back to Africa."

After a little more talk Zachary admitted the real reason he was going was to get away from his father. Mr. Young had made him quit school to work in the mill. "Don't look so unhappy," Zachary said before he left. "I'll be home in no time. And I won't really be fighting. I'll just be beating on a drum and running errands."

Joseph tossed and turned in his bed that night, his head too crowded with thoughts to sleep. Sometimes the war did sound exciting. Maybe what he really hated was the way the war was already changing everything. A few weeks ago he had been going to school and spending all his free time with Zachary and David at the cave. It was summer now, but there were rumors the school would not start again until the war was over because so many of the teachers had joined the army. Joseph hadn't cared all that much about school when he went every day, but now it seemed a terrible loss.

Mr. Byers had returned home safely at last. Joseph heard sounds from the kitchen as his mother prepared a late supper. He heard the murmur of voices and knew that his mother was passing on Zachary's warning. Joseph knew it wouldn't do any good. Mr. Byers was a stubborn man. He wouldn't let the threat of trouble stop him from doing what he thought was right.

Joseph wondered what his stepfather was going to do with all the pamphlets they had printed that afternoon. If he passed them out to the townspeople, there would be more trouble.

It was nearly morning when Joseph finally slipped into an uneasy sleep. It seemed he had no more than closed his eyes when he was awakened by Jared tugging at his blankets. "Get up, Joseph," Jared said. "Papa says it's late, and you haven't done the morning milking."

Although Joseph could not yet bring himself to call Mr. Byers Papa, Jared had no such reservations.

"Tell him I'm up," Joseph said without moving. He groaned. His eyelids felt puffy, and he wanted nothing better than to curl up and go back to sleep. Then he remembered Zachary's visit the night before and jumped out of bed. Zachary's train left at noon, and he had promised to go to the depot and see him off.

Jared trailed after Joseph while he got dressed and ate a quick breakfast. "Can I go with you to the train?" he asked. From across the kitchen Mrs. Byers looked alarmed and shook her head. "It's a long walk," Joseph said, "and it's going to be hot. Besides, people in town are not very friendly these days."

Jared's thin face looked sad. Joseph knelt beside him. "I'll tell you what," he said. "I have some little pieces of wood left from when I carved your wagon. When I get home, I'll make you some boxes and barrels to go with it."

His brother nodded solemnly. "I'd like that."

As soon as he had done the milking and filled the firebox with wood, Joseph headed for town. He stopped at David's house on the way. "We have not seen thee for several days," David's mother said.

As usual the Quaker family's house was full of the smell of baking. Mrs. Baker insisted that Joseph come in and eat a warm sticky bun fresh from the oven. When he entered the kitchen, Hannah jumped up and tried to hide the slate of spelling words she had been copying. She gave a sigh of relief when she saw it was Joseph. "You scared me," she said. "I was studying so hard, I didn't hear you arrive."

Joseph looked at her slate. "You are almost caught up to our level," he said.

"Mrs. Baker is a good teacher," Hannah replied.

Mrs. Baker smiled at Hannah. "Thou are a good student."

Joseph told David and Hannah the news about Zachary. "He wants to be free of his father," David said. "But perhaps this choice will prove to be even worse."

"Mama sent me to pick up Mrs. Taggert's wash," Hannah said. "I'd better go before she gets worried." At the door she stopped and said wistfully, "Do you ever go to the cave anymore?"

Joseph shook his head. "Now that school is out, I'm afraid someone will follow us and find it."

David wrapped one of the buns in a cloth napkin and handed it to Hannah. "Take this in case thou get hungry later."

Hannah picked up her empty basket and hurried off in one direction while the boys headed in the opposite direction toward the train station at the edge of town. As usual, the people they passed on the street gave them unfriendly stares. Folks were gathered on every street corner, exchanging information about the war. "England is sure to help the South," one man loudly proclaimed to anyone who would listen. "They need our cotton for their mills."

The train was already at the platform when the boys arrived. They squeezed their way through throngs of people all bidding loved ones good-bye. Many waved hastily sewn Confederate flags. "Do thou see Zachary?" David asked.

"Yes, I see him," Joseph shouted eagerly. Zachary was hanging out one of the windows on the train, frantically waving to get their attention.

"I thought no one going to see me off," Zachary said when they managed to reach him.

"I didn't know there would be so many people," Joseph exclaimed.

"I didn't either," Zachary said with a grin. "Makes a person feel downright important." He shouted to make himself heard over the lively music of the brass band standing near the tracks.

Several women pushed through the crowd. Their wide skirts took up half the platform. One of them dabbed her eyes with a dainty white handkerchief. "Don't cry," a young man told her. "We'll whop those Yankees and be back home in no time." He was one of the fortunate few to be wearing a uniform. It was a crisp dark blue.

David nudged Joseph. "How will anyone know he's not in the Union army with that uniform? The Confederate uniform is supposed to be gray!"

A rousing cheer went up at the young man's words. "Them Yankees are nothing but shopkeepers," yelled a rosy-cheeked boy. He too was wearing a uniform. It had obviously been made at home, possibly by his mother. It was more a butternut brown than gray, but at least it didn't look like a Yankee uniform.

David handed Zachary a package. "My mother made a lunch for thee in case thou get hungry during the ride."

"Tell your mother I'm grateful," Zachary shouted as the train slowly started to move. He glanced at the crowd, trying to hide his disappointment that his father had not even come to wave good-bye.

Joseph searched his pockets frantically for a parting gift. His fingers closed on a round brass medal he had received for winning the school spelling bee. "Here," he said, handing it to Zachary. The train was moving, and he had to run alongside it to keep up. "Keep that for good luck."

Zachary pinned the medal to his shirt. "I'll give it back to you when I come home." He waved a final time as the train picked up more speed.

After the passenger cars came car after car of goods. "The Yankees are blocking the river," Joseph overheard a man say. "So far, though, they haven't tried to stop the trains from hauling supplies to the South."

The crowd drifted away. Their mood was less jovial than it had been a few minutes before. The

band members slowly packed away their instruments. Suddenly a horseback rider galloped by the station. He pulled hard on the reins to stop his mount and waved a telegram as he shouted to the crowd. "There's been a battle at a place called Manassas Junction. We beat them. The Yankees ran all the way home!"

EIGHT

Fire!

The train station and in fact the whole town erupted in celebration. The band members took out their instruments again and led a parade down the main street. "I knew those Yankees would turn tail and run," a man shouted.

"We should just keep on going and capture Washington," yelled another.

"General Beauregard had his Confederate troops dug in around a creek called Bull Run," Joseph heard the man who had delivered the news explain to the crowd. "He was waiting for them."

"That's just where Mr. Byers said they would fight," Joseph said. "Mama said he was a soldier a long time ago. I guess that's how he knew."

70
★

"Looks like the war will be over before Zachary gets to Tennessee," David exclaimed.

Joseph saw Aunt Bea standing by the general store with her shopping basket. Aunt Bea was Mayor Cooper's slave. She was his cook, and her pies were so delicious they were known throughout the county. Aunt Bea was a large woman with a round face that was always smiling. She wasn't smiling now, however. She put her shopping basket down on the wooden sidewalk and stood watching the crowd with a look Joseph could not decipher.

A man watching the merrymakers bumped into Aunt Bea. He turned with an angry look until he saw who it was.

Aunt Bea apologized for the collision, even though she was not to blame. The man waved his hand, brushing aside her apology without admitting his fault. "Why, Aunt Bea," he said pleasantly, "you still making those delicious pies?"

"Oh, yes, sir," Aunt Bea said, her face smoothed out into a broad smile. "I surely am."

"I bought me a new gal last month. She could use

a few cooking lessons. Suppose you could teach her if I brought her over to you?"

"If Massa Cooper says it's all right, then I suppose I could," Aunt Bea answered.

"You tell the mayor I'll be over to see him soon," the man said as he continued on his way. Every trace of smile was gone as Aunt Bea watched him disappear into the crowd. After a minute she hurried up the street.

Joseph stared after her for a long time. "The slaves really hate us, don't they?" he said.

"Some do," David said. "Can thou blame them?"

The boys trudged homeward in silence. Finally, David said, "It grieves me that Zachary has joined with the Confederates to defend slavery."

Joseph felt compelled to support his friend. "He says this war is about states' rights. His captain told him the Constitution gave the states the right to rule themselves and now the federal government is trying to take that away."

David gave him a sideways look. "States' rights to do what? Keep people as slaves? At any rate, the Constitution says, " 'We the people,' not 'We the states.' The states willingly agreed to be a country. They can't leave the Union every time they disagree."

Joseph was still wrestling with that question. At last year's Fourth of July celebration, the bands marched and there were patriotic speeches. The sight of the flag filled him with a proud feeling. Yet if he'd been asked, he would have called himself a southerner.

"Do you think Kentucky will be able to stay out of this war?" Joseph asked.

David shook his head. "My father says sooner or later it will have to make a choice."

"Mr. Byers says that more of the state is for the Union than for the Confederacy," Joseph said. "It sure doesn't seem that way in Branson Mills."

"The family next door has two sons who went off to fight for the North," David said. "Now Mrs. Iverson across the street says they should cross their names out of the family Bible and say they have no sons. She says in a battle those boys could be shooting at her son. Before all this started, they were good friends."

"You're lucky your family are Quakers," Joseph said. "You don't have to worry about what side you are on."

"We don't believe in fighting our fellowman," David said gently. "That doesn't mean we don't consider what is right or wrong." He hesitated. "It's not easy to uphold our beliefs. Andrew has called me a coward."

Joseph looked at his friend. "Didn't that make you angry?"

David nodded. "My father tells me it is braver not to fight." He smiled. "But sometimes I think it would be nice not to be a Quaker for just a few minutes."

Late that night Joseph was awakened suddenly. It was a sticky, hot night, and he was sweating in his bedclothes. He got up and crossed the room to the window. When he drew open the curtains, the room was bathed in moonlight. He pushed open his window to let in some air and stumbled back to bed. He heard laughter and the sound of horses' hooves on the street. Several loud cracks of gunfire, sounding very near, made him freeze in terror. Trembling, he crept downstairs.

Mr. Byers was sitting by the window, watching the street. No candles were lit, but enough light came through for Joseph to see the gun on the floor beside his stepfather.

When Mr. Byers heard Joseph, he spoke without turning away from the window. "Go back to bed. It's just a noisy group celebrating the victory."

"I thought we were being attacked," Joseph said. He sighed with relief.

Joseph's mother appeared at the top of the stairs in her nightdress. Her hair, usually wrapped in two buns, one over each ear, tumbled down to her waist in curls. Without her wide skirts she seemed tiny, almost frail. Joseph noted with surprise that he had grown taller than his mother. "Do you think they will come here?" Mrs. Byers asked fearfully.

"I thought they might," Mr. Byers replied. "But they seem content to ride around and shoot their guns in the air."

"Are you coming to bed?" Mrs. Byers asked.

"It's nearly morning. I suppose it's safe enough," answered Mr. Byers, turning around at last. Even in the dim light Joseph could see the strain on his face.

Suddenly a clanging bell could be heard over the din of the revelers. "Fire!" exclaimed Mr. Byers. He rushed out on the porch and looked toward town.

"Those fools have set something on fire," he said. Joseph followed him out. A faint glow lit up the sky. "I'd better go," Mr. Byers said grimly. "It will take every hand available, from the looks of it."

"I should go too," Joseph said. "I'm big enough to help."

Mr. Byers gave him an appraising look. At last he nodded. "Get dressed. And hurry."

Joseph nearly flew upstairs. He yanked on his pants and shirt and jammed his feet into shoes.

His stepfather handed Joseph a large, sturdy bucket. He picked up one for himself.

His mother had wrapped a shawl around her shoulders. "Be careful," she said in a small voice.

Mr. Byers turned back from the door. "I'm sure no one will come now. I will leave the gun just in case."

Mrs. Byers shivered in spite of the warm night, but she nodded.

His stepfather set off at such a fast walk, Joseph had to run to keep up. The empty bucket clanged against his leg. Here and there other men and boys came out of their houses and headed for town. Branson Mills was fortunate to have the river so close by. But it did not have a pumper as did many of the larger cities. When there was a fire, a line was formed to pass buckets of water from the river. Sometimes in the case of a serious fire there was little anyone could do except to keep it from spreading. There were a few brick buildings in Branson Mills, but most of them were frame. They would catch quickly, especially after the dry spring.

The scene downtown was like a nightmare. Thick billows of greasy smoke rolled out of Mr. Byers's factory. Flames shot from the roof and the windows, which were already cracked from the heat. Two long lines had been formed leading to the river. Buckets of water passed from hand to hand in the first line, and empty buckets returned in the second. The heat was so intense that the water seemed to have little effect. It sizzled into steam the minute it hit the flames. Already several of the stores nearby were burning.

A groan escaped Mr. Byers when he saw the remains of his factory. It was obvious that it could not be saved. He whirled around, looking at the other buildings in town. Suddenly he sprang into action.

"Forget the factory," he shouted over the roar of the flames. "We need to wet down some of these other buildings before the whole town burns."

For an instant it seemed the men would ignore him. Then Sheriff Underwood grabbed a bucket of water and threw it on Mr. Abernathy's drugstore. "He's right. Come on, men!"

Joseph, awed by the force of the flames, had been frozen in place. Now he jumped into action beside the other men and boys and even a few women. New lines formed as more and more men arrived. The smoke made it difficult to breathe. Joseph coughed, and his eyes ran in a steady stream of tears. It was as if the fire were something alive. No sooner would it seem they were winning the fight than flames would erupt from another building.

Bucket after bucket passed through Joseph's hands until his shoulders ached.

"Step out of line and take a rest, boy," said the man next to him. "There's plenty of others to take your place."

It was Mr. Curtis, hardly recognizable with a thick coating of soot covering his face. Joseph wondered if his own face looked the same.

"I'm all right," Joseph grunted. In truth he wanted nothing more than to sit down and rest.

A warm wind briefly blew the smoke away from his face. Gratefully, Joseph breathed deeply. But the breeze stirred up the fire, making it spread even more.

The roof of his stepfather's factory fell in with a shower of sparks. Joseph looked for Mr. Byers. Finally he spotted him working with an ax, clearing some rubble. He'd seen his brother Clay in another bucket line earlier. Some people had even brought their slaves to help fight the fire.

The wind grew stronger. Huge pieces of burning ash blew in the air, starting other fires when they landed.

"The newspaper office is on fire," screamed Mr. Healey. Joseph saw David join the line formed to fight the new fire. By dawn it seemed that everyone in town was there. He saw Hannah's father and Mr. Baker working side by side, wetting down the stable. Mr. Curtis had led the frightened horses away earlier, but it looked as though the stable would be spared.

It was well into the morning, and still the fire was not under control. Other men came, relieving them for a few minutes. Some women set up a table with coffee cakes and rolls, coffee and water.

Joseph took a sweet roll and coffee and sat close to the river, away from the smoke. He was almost too weary to eat. His hands stung with newly formed blisters and tiny burns from flying sparks.

Mrs. Lippit was crying. "Our beautiful town. How did this happen?"

"I heard someone started a fire in the Byers factory," another woman answered, "but it got out of control."

Mayor Cooper came by and stuffed several rolls in his pocket. Joseph noticed that his face was not nearly as dirty as the other men's. No one seemed to notice Joseph sitting by himself with his back to a tree.

"Do you know who did it?" Mrs. Lippit asked.

The mayor helped himself to another roll. He shook his head, making the great jowls of fat under his chin swing from side to side. "Not yet," he said around a huge mouthful. "I heard that factory was full of abolitionist literature. Stacks and stacks of it."

Joseph sat up straighter. How did Mayor Cooper know that the pamphlets were in the factory?

"I heard about your trouble with Aunt Bea," one of the women said.

Mayor Cooper nodded solemnly. "I had to whip her. I let her off with only five lashes. But I'll leave her wearing shackles for a few months. That will cure any more ideas of running off."

"It's that sort of thing that makes me know we are right to keep them slaves. Those people just don't think like we do. Here you've taken care of her all these years and she tries to run off," Mrs. Lippit remarked.

Mayor Cooper chuckled. "It's a lucky thing for her she is such a good cook." Suddenly noticing Joseph, he fell silent.

Joseph did not speak. He could feel their eyes watching him as he stood up and walked to the bucket line without a backward glance.

NINE

Some Important Decisions

By late in the morning the fire was out. Mr. Byers's factory was little more than a pile of sodden ashes. The whole town looked as if it had been the scene of a terrible war. At least four other businesses had burned to the ground, and many more were damaged. Thick, acrid smoke still filled the air.

Several boys Joseph had known in school were leaning against Mr. Abernathy's drugstore. They had been part of the group that had harassed him about his stepfather's work to free the slaves. Now they raised a hand in greeting. At least the fire had made everyone forget the animosities. For a time they had been united against an even bigger enemy than one another.

83

"Joseph," a voice called. It was Hannah. She was passing out dippers of cold water to the exhausted firefighters. The boys were watching. One of them smirked and said something in a low voice to the others. Joseph turned away, pretending he hadn't seen Hannah. He was sick with shame at his cowardice, but he couldn't make himself speak to her. Not with everyone watching. Out of the corner of his eye he saw her hurt expression as she stared after him. Feeling as if every eye in town were upon him, Joseph walked away briskly, hoping she would not follow. He risked a quick glance as he turned the corner. Hannah was standing in the same spot, looking forlorn. The boys were still watching. He searched for his stepfather and finally spotted him standing alone, staring at the rubble. His clothes were filthy, and the wrinkles in his face were lined with soot, making him look much older than he was. Joseph felt suddenly ashamed. He had been too weak to acknowledge his friendship with Hannah, yet his stepfather had lost everything because of his beliefs.

Mr. Byers roused himself and even managed a

half smile. "Let's go home," he said. "Your mama is probably awful worried."

Joseph nodded gratefully. They trudged home, too tired for conversation. They found Joseph's mother waiting for them on the porch. Jared was tucked on the porch swing beside her. She jumped up anxiously to meet them.

"Everything is lost," Mr. Byers mumbled.

Silently she hugged them both, then insisted they eat and take hot baths before they staggered off to sleep. Joseph crawled into bed, hardly aware when his mother covered him with a soft coverlet and kissed his forehead. The next thing he knew, sun was flooding his room and it was a new day.

"You slept a long time," Jared announced when Joseph hurried downstairs. "I wanted to wake you up, but Mama wouldn't let me."

"Did anyone milk Daisy?" Joseph asked worriedly.

Jared grinned. "Mama did. And I helped."

"Good for you!" Joseph exclaimed.

"It was fun," Jared said. "Clay wanted to do it, but Mama said I was a good enough helper."

"Clay's here?" Joseph was pleased. He had caught

glimpses of his brother during the fire, but there had been no chance to talk.

Now, Joseph heard Clay's voice in the kitchen. "I was about ready to check if you were still alive," his brother said when he walked in. He rubbed the top of Joseph's head with one knuckle in a brotherly show of affection.

"Ow." Joseph grimaced. "What are you doing here?"

"I just came to say good-bye," Clay said. "Dr. Mercer and I are heading over to Virginia to see if we can be of help."

Mrs. Byers looked distraught. "I don't want you near the fighting."

"The fighting is over," Clay said. "Dr. Mercer knows a doctor in Virginia who has some interesting new ideas. He wants to talk to him about Jared. Since we are going to be there anyway, we'll see if we can help with the wounded men. Dr. Mercer thinks it will be good practice in case there is any fighting here. The paper says the Union lost more than nine hundred men, and a lot more were wounded. They will need all the help they can get."

After he had eaten, Joseph spread a newspaper on the table and picked up his knife and a small piece of wood. Carefully he began to whittle as he listened to the conversation. Jared came over to watch. Slowly a small round barrel emerged from the wood.

"You sure have a talent for that," Clay said, holding the carving up and admiring it.

"It needs some smoothing out," said Joseph, pleased at his brother's praise.

"I almost forgot," Clay said. "Mr. Johnson at the general store said to tell you he sold that eagle you carved. An army officer bought it for his desk. He paid thirty dollars for it."

"Congratulations," Mr. Byers said warmly. "That is a goodly sum of money for a boy."

Joseph shrugged. "I don't need it. Mr. Johnson will take five dollars for selling it, but that will leave twenty-five dollars."

"That will buy food for us for a month," said Mr. Byers. "It will give me some time to think about what to do."

"Maybe I could get a job," Joseph said.

Mr. Byers shook his head. "You are needed at home, Joseph." He sat beside his wife and gently held her hands. "I truly believe no country can become great while holding part of its people in bondage. I also do not believe that the states have the right to break away from the Union simply so they can continue this practice. I've been doing a lot of talking, but others who feel the same way are fighting for their beliefs."

As though she understood what he was going to say next, Mrs. Byers shook her head. "This is a young man's war. We need you here."

Joseph's stepfather let go of his wife's hands and stood up. He paced the floor as he went on speaking. "Do you remember I told you I was a graduate of West Point? In those days there was only a small army and too many officers. So I resigned my commission after a few years. I am going to ask to be reinstated. If I am accepted, I would be a captain in the Union army."

A stunned silence followed this announcement. "My brothers will join the southern army," Mrs. Byers said softly.

"And Zachary," Joseph blurted out.

Mr. Byers looked anguished. "I cannot fight against my beliefs. You knew when I married you that I was against slavery."

"I didn't know that you would make everyone in town our enemy," Mrs. Byers said coldly. "It's all very well for you. You have your abolitionist friends. I notice they stay hidden well enough. Their wives don't get shunned at church. Their sons are not attacked on the street by hoodlums."

Joseph looked up in surprise. How had she found out?

Mr. Byers looked pained, but Joseph's mother did not back down. Joseph had never seen her so angry.

"My abolitionist friends stay hidden so they can help slaves on the Underground Railroad," Mr. Byers said at last. "I am sorry this is so hard for my family."

Joseph's mother did not speak. Mr. Byers continued to pace. "With the factory gone, I have no way to support my family. If I joined the Confederates, I would be fighting against everything I believe."

Without another word Mrs. Byers stood up to

leave. Her skirts swished against the door as she left the room.

"I'll tell Dr. Mercer I need to return home," Clay said in a strained voice.

"No, Clay," Mr. Byers said heavily. "Being a doctor is important work. I think this country will have great need of your services. It will take some time to get an answer. If I do go, Sheriff Underwood has promised to watch out for the family, and Joseph can take care of the chores. I suspect people will be kinder if I am not here."

"Everyone thinks the war will be over quickly," Clay said. "The South is sure to win. Look what happened at Manassas."

Mr. Byers shook his head. "General McDowell did not have time to train his army properly. I've read reports of the battle. It was a disaster. The Rebels slipped in more troops on the Manassas Gap Railroad, so they arrived fresh and ready to fight. There was some confusion over uniforms too," Mr. Byers added. "Some of the Confederates had blue uniforms just like the North's."

"Dr. Mercer says the Congress is calling for half a

million men to serve three years," Clay told them. "President Lincoln gave the job of training them to General McClellan."

"I hope he does better than McDowell," said Mr. Byers. "He was so sure of winning, he even invited civilians to watch. They got in the way and added to the panic. I've heard good things about McClellan. But the South has good leaders. A lot of the top army officers left the North and joined the Confederate army. That's another reason I feel I must go."

"People in Branson Mills will call you a traitor," Joseph blurted out.

"And you, Joseph, how will you feel?"

"I don't know," Joseph whispered.

Clay glared at his brother. "I would join the Federals if I were older."

"Thank God you are not," Mr. Byers said quietly.

Dinner that night was stewed chicken with noodles, crusty bread warm from the oven, and a pot of strawberry jam. Even though it was everyone's favorite dinner, tonight they all picked at their food and finally pushed back their plates half full. Clay left right after dinner when Mr. Byers assured him once again the family would be all right without him. Mrs. Byers did not speak to her husband. She put Jared to bed and started heating water to wash dishes. Mr. Byers sighed heavily as he walked outside to sit on the porch. It was a fine summer evening, and a cool breeze came in from the open door. It carried the smell of smoke from town, reminding Joseph of the terrible fight against the flames. It was a night when a person should feel glad just to be alive, but Joseph could not find one thing to make him smile.

TEN

A Summer Day

It was a hot summer. Day after day of baking sun was broken briefly by short, violent thunderstorms that only made it sticky. His mother sat in the parlor, fanning herself with a lacy paper fan, and Mr. Byers was grimly silent. Joseph forced himself to get up early and get his chores done before the weather became unbearable. Even so, by the time he had milked Daisy, weeded the garden, and split the kindling, he was drenched with sweat.

It seemed as if everyone was waiting for something. President Lincoln waited to see if Kentucky would remain neutral or finally choose a side. The North waited for General McClellan to turn the thousands of untrained soldiers who had shamed themselves at Bull Run into a proper army. The South waited for another resounding victory. At home there was waiting too. Mr. Byers waited for an answer to his letter, and Mrs. Byers waited and worried about Clay. Joseph waited for life to return to normal, to the way it was before the war divided the country and his home.

The railroad bridge was finished, and trains once again ran north, though there were frequent delays. Armed men patrolled both bridges. They had organized themselves and were now called the Home Guard.

There was another group of men, though no one seemed to know who they were. They called themselves the Vengeance Committee. Anyone for the Union could expect a visit from the committee sooner or later. Families who had sons fighting for the Union awoke to find burning garbage on their porches. David Baker woke up one morning to find the word *traitor* painted in large letters across the front of his house and his mother's carefully tended vegetable garden destroyed.

Mrs. Byers thinned her garden and packed plants

in baskets. "You take these to David's house and help replant them," she said to Joseph.

He found David already at work, trying to rescue the few plants that could be saved. David's eyebrows went up in surprise to see him.

"Thou are a good friend," David said as he took one of the heavy baskets from Joseph.

"It was my mother's idea," Joseph mumbled. "But I'll stay and help you plant."

David nodded. Together they worked away the afternoon, carefully replanting and then carrying buckets of water from the well and dipping out a cupful for each new seedling.

When they were done, the garden looked nearly as good as before the visit from the Vengeance Committee.

"What if it happens again?" Joseph asked.

"Father says we shall tie Juno near the garden each night. At least she will give some warning." Juno was Abe's sister, also a gift from Hannah.

Joseph was still worried. "Your father will not fight. Even if Juno gives a warning, what will he do?"

David winked. "My father has a plan," he said as they walked to the house. "Since there was no Fourth of July celebration this year, we did not use all the firecrackers we had. We are going to string them together. Any intruders will think there's an army protecting this garden."

Mr. Baker was applying a fresh coat of paint to the front of the house. David's mother looked out the door. "Are thou hungry?" she asked. "Thou have done a good day's work."

Joseph nodded. "Yes, ma'am. I believe I am." The good smells coming from the kitchen made him feel dizzy with hunger.

They washed up at the pump and tramped into the house for dinner. Hannah was there, helping Mrs. Baker. Her schoolbooks were stacked neatly on the table.

"Hello, Joseph," she said shyly.

"Hannah has made dinner tonight almost by herself," announced Mr. Baker.

"I thank thee for the warning," David teased.

"Ha," Hannah snorted. "I should like to see you do as well."

Joseph felt envious of their easy banter. Obviously Hannah was an accepted part of the Baker household.

Dinner at the Bakers' house was not as formal as at his own. After grace the family conversed easily and encouraged Joseph to join in. The dinner was excellent too: a chicken pie with chunks of meat and tender vegetables covered with a light, flaky crust. With it there were garden greens and plump soft biscuits.

After dinner David dug out a baseball and bat, and they practiced batting in a field near the house. Several other neighborhood children stopped by. They came in twos and threes, and soon there were enough to form teams and have a real game. Some looked surprised to see Hannah, but after a few minutes of watching her play, each side wanted her on its team. They played until the fireflies came out and it was too dark to see the ball. For a time on that hot summer night, black or white, Confederate or Union mattered not a bit.

When they returned to the Bakers' house, Mrs. Baker poured cream, sugar, and fresh raspberries in a container. This she placed in a wooden churn packed with ice and salt. Everyone took turns cranking the handle until at last she poured out bowls of soft, cool ice cream.

"This is delicious!" Joseph exclaimed.

"I will give thee some to take home to thy family," Mrs. Baker said. She packed a large bowl for Joseph to take home.

Joseph carried it carefully and was rewarded by the smiles of pleasure as Jared spooned up a large helping. Joseph's mother and Mr. Byers took small bowlfuls also. While they ate, Joseph told them about his day.

"Hannah is really amazing," he said. "Mrs. Baker says she has been teaching her for only about a year, but she is almost caught up with David and me."

Mrs. Byers licked her spoon and sighed with pleasure, but Mr. Byers seemed distracted. Finally he pushed his bowl away. "You speak of Hannah as if she were your equal," he said to Joseph.

Taken aback, Joseph could only stammer, "Well, she is."

Mr. Byers nodded and spoke softly, almost to himself. "It's strange. I've fought against slavery all these years because I felt it was wrong. And it is. And I suppose I imagined that when the slaves were free some would return to Africa and the others . . ." He shrugged. "Well, they would work as they always have, but they would be fairly paid and free to leave a master who beat them. Of course I knew that many were fine craftsmen, but still, they could never be our *equals*." Mr. Byers took a drink of his coffee. "Now here is Hannah—your equal, as you say, in hard work, courage, and learning."

Mr. Byers raised his voice. "It was bad enough to keep the black people slaves if they were lesser humans as we have believed. But if Hannah is an example of what they can do if they are free, how much worse is our crime!"

Mr. Byers chuckled, seeing their wide eyes at his fiery outburst. "I guess I thought I was beginning one of my speeches." He paused. "This is as good a time to tell you as any," he said. "I've received an answer to my letter. I am to leave for Washington next week."

ELEVEN

———◆———

The Vengeance Committee

The next day Mr. Byers unpacked his uniform from a trunk in the attic and was pleased to see that it still fit. He cleaned and oiled the long, slender sword that fastened at his side. Joseph thought he looked very dashing. Mr. Byers talked with Joseph's mother through the day. After her original shock, she seemed to have accepted his decision, and they spent most of the time going over household accounts.

Joseph was left to entertain Jared. After dinner they lined up a set of tin soldiers and pretended to have a war. Suddenly Jared pushed all the soldiers over. "I don't want Papa to go," he said.

"Maybe the war will be over soon and he can come home," Joseph said.

"Will you miss him?" Jared asked.

Joseph nodded, suddenly realizing it was true.

Jared gave him a reproachful stare. "Then you should call him Papa."

Joseph laughed. "I will someday."

Looking relieved, Jared went off to bed. Joseph took out his carving, intending to make several more pieces of freight for his brother's toy wagon. Mrs. Byers was in the kitchen. After waiting several hours for the bread dough to rise, she punched it back down and shaped it into loaves ready to bake for the next day's bread. Mr. Byers was sitting on the porch, enjoying the slightly cooler evening air.

Suddenly Abe barked a sharp warning. At the same time, Joseph heard angry shouting and the thud of feet on the porch. Alarmed, he dropped his carving and ran to the door. Out of the corner of his eye he saw his mother running from the kitchen, a white towel still in her hands.

It took Joseph a minute to realize what he was seeing when he stepped out on the porch. Three men were dragging Mr. Byers off the porch. They were dressed in work clothes, and a black hood covered each of their faces. The hoods had eyeholes cut out, giving them a ghostly appearance. A fourth man sat in the driver's seat of a wagon stopped in front of the house. A hood also hid his face. Mr. Byers was struggling fiercely, but the men had managed to tie his hands behind his back, and one of them was roughly fastening a gag around his mouth.

Except for Mr. Byers's angry shouts when he was first captured, the entire struggle was silent.

Even as he stood horror-stuck at what he was seeing, it passed through Joseph's mind that the men were silent because they were afraid they would be recognized if they spoke.

At last Joseph came to his senses and flung himself at the nearest hoodlum. "Leave him alone," he shouted. He was a whirlwind of anger, hitting the man with his fists and kicking with all his strength.

From the doorway he heard his mother's cry. "What are you doing to my husband?"

The bully Joseph was attacking suddenly had enough and with little effort threw Joseph back against the porch wall. His head hit the wall with a sickening thud, and for a moment his vision was blocked with shooting points of light. Mrs. Byers reached him just as his head cleared and he struggled to sit up.

One of the men hesitated. "We have no quarrel with you, ma'am," he said in an obviously disguised voice. "The boy neither. We don't much like abolitionists in this town stirring up all the darkies. Your husband's been warned enough times. You can call us the Vengeance Committee."

"I would rather call you cowards," Mrs. Byers said furiously.

The masked man seemed about to say more but thought better of it. He held Mrs. Byers back while the other men continued to bind and gag her husband. Joseph stared at them, trying to get some clue to their identity. There was something vaguely familiar about the man's voice, even with his attempt to change it.

"Hurry up," the driver growled.

The three men dragged Mr. Byers down the steps and threw him into the wagon. They had barely enough time to climb on board themselves before

the driver cracked his whip and drove the wagon away at breakneck speed.

Joseph struggled to get up, but his mother held him back. "Let me go," he shouted. "We've got to stop them." He looked bitterly at the nearby houses. Although light flickered through most of the windows, no one came to their aid. Did they really not hear, or did they just not want to hear?

Mrs. Byers shook his arm. "There is nothing you can do against all those men. Run and get Sheriff Underwood. He'll know what to do."

Joseph stood up and was immediately dizzy. His body swayed for a minute before he could clear his head. "Are you hurt?" his mother cried. She reached up to touch his head.

"I'm fine," Joseph lied. He felt a trickle of warm blood on his forehead. "It's just a scratch."

He dashed down the stairs and ran to the street. Sheriff Underwood's house was close to town so that he could care for any prisoners in the jail. Usually there was no one more dangerous than a farmer who'd had too much to drink on a Saturday night or a couple of fellows fighting over some girl who probably didn't care about either one of them. On those occasions the sheriff's wife cooked them dinner, and he released them after they had a night to cool down.

Joseph's feet pounded on the rough pavement. It was almost a shock seeing the town again. Although some cleanup work had already been done, the place had a dismal, dirty look.

He was gasping for breath, and there was a stitch in his side. His head hurt, but he wouldn't stop. Tears formed in his eyes as he thought about what might be happening to his stepfather even now. He flew past the dry goods store and the train station. He was sobbing by the time he reached the sheriff's neat frame house. It had not been damaged, although one wall of the jail had been scorched. A narrow porch ran along the front of the house. He raced up the porch stairs and banged on the door.

"Sheriff Underwood," Joseph cried. "Hurry. They've taken Mr. Byers."

The sheriff opened the door. "What is that you are saying? Who has taken him? Calm down, boy. Tell me what happened."

"It's the Vengeance Committee. Four men,"

Joseph gasped. "They tied him up and took him away in a wagon."

The sheriff frowned. "Four men, you say? Which way did they go?"

"North, I think," Joseph answered. "Hurry, please," he sobbed.

The sheriff patted Joseph. "Don't worry. We'll find him. But I'm going to need some help." He said a few quiet words to his wife and walked quickly next door to the jail. Joseph ran after him. He was growing more anxious at each passing moment.

Tom, the sheriff's deputy, jumped up from the desk where he'd been reading the newspaper by the light of a coal oil lamp. Tom was a huge man who hardly ever spoke. "We've got trouble," Sheriff Underwood said. "Go get Pete and Amos Hardy, and be quick."

Tom nodded and ran out the door. "Shouldn't we ring the fire bell?" Joseph asked. The bell was on a pole outside the jail and could be used to summon help in an emergency.

Sheriff Underwood shook his head. "No sense to advertise that we are coming. Anyway, it would take too long to get everyone here and form a posse. You'd better get home and help your ma."

From the single jail cell came a sleepy voice. "I could help. Mr. Byers has always treated me fine."

"Well, Jeb," said the sheriff, "if you were a sober man, I'd take you up on that." He unlocked a gun cabinet and took out four shotguns.

Old Jeb, who spent more nights in the jail than out of it, was silent. A moment later Joseph heard a rumbling snore. Under other circumstances it would have been funny. Now the sound just filled him with despair. "Can't I go with you?" he asked.

"No," the sheriff said sharply. "You get on home." Then in a kinder voice he said, "Your ma will need someone for company while she waits. She's probably beside herself by now. She doesn't need to be worrying about you too."

Tom soon returned with two grim-faced men. "Horses are ready around the back," he said. The guns were quickly handed out, and the men rode out at a hard gallop. Joseph ran after them, but he couldn't keep up. In a few minutes the riders had disappeared into the dark night.

TWELVE

———◆———

A Long Night

Instead of returning directly home, Joseph ran to David's house. The windows were dark, and Joseph had to knock several times before a thin light appeared at an upstairs window. "Who is there?" Mr. Baker called down.

"It's Joseph. I'm sorry to bother you, but something terrible has happened."

"Wait there," Mr. Baker said. A second later he appeared at the door, tucking his nightshirt into his pants. Mrs. Baker and David crowded down the stairs behind him.

"Tell me what has happened," Mr. Baker said in his calm, quiet way. He listened intently while Joseph told the story.

"Thy poor mother," exclaimed Mrs. Baker. "As soon as I dress, I shall come to see if I can give some comfort."

David gave Joseph a sympathetic look. "Do thou also need a friend this night?"

Joseph nodded, too weary to speak. The Bakers quickly dressed, and together they walked down the dark streets to Joseph's home.

Mrs. Byers was waiting at the door, anxiously peering out into the night. She sagged with relief when she saw Joseph. She hugged him tight. "You were gone so long, I feared something had happened to you too."

"We should like to stay with thee," Mrs. Baker said. "Perhaps we can be of some help."

Joseph's mother nodded. "I'd be grateful for your company."

Mrs. Baker went to the kitchen and a few minutes later brought out steaming cups of coffee. Mrs. Byers took a few sips and went back to the window. She stared out at the darkness. "I begged him not to speak out so much," she moaned, wringing her hands. "First his business is burned, and now this."

"Thy husband is a brave man," Mr. Baker said. "We shall pray for his safe return." He took his wife's hand, and she in turn held Joseph's. Around the table their hands made an unbroken circle, and they bowed their heads.

The next few hours were the longest that Joseph had ever spent. No one spoke much. Joseph listened to each tick of the parlor clock as the time crept by. Occasionally he drifted off to sleep, only to wake a few minutes later with a guilty start. Mrs. Byers spent most of her time pacing the floor or peering out the window at the silent, empty street.

"Why is it taking so long?" she moaned.

At last, just as the first streaks of light appeared on the horizon, they heard the clatter of horses' hooves out on the street.

Joseph and his mother rushed to the door in time to see three horses stop in front of the house. Two men were on the sheriff's horse. The man in front weaved in the saddle and would have fallen if the sheriff had not put out a hand to restrain him. The sheriff wearily dismounted and assisted Mr. Byers off the horse. The two deputies slid off their horses and supported Mr. Byers as he walked to the door. Mrs. Byers nearly fainted at the first sight of her husband. In the dim light he appeared to be covered with blood. Closer inspection in the lamplight, however, showed the spots to be tar.

He had been badly beaten. His eyes were swollen shut, and there were cuts over his body. They took him inside and gently sat him in a chair.

"Sorry, ma'am," a deputy said. "I wish we could have gotten there in time to stop this."

"Makes me shamed to be a human," said the sheriff. "Take a man out of his own house and do a cowardly thing like this just because you don't agree with him."

"Did you catch them?" Joseph burst out.

The sheriff shook his head. "Sorry, son. They slunk off through the woods. We chased them a bit but thought we'd better get Mr. Byers home. Tom's still out there looking, but I think they have given us the slip."

"One of them might be Mr. Young," Joseph said. He told them of Zachary's warning.

"I wouldn't put it past Young. That man is meaner than a snake," said Sheriff Underwood. He turned to the deputies. "You two check out Young. See if he is home. And check his buggy horses. See if they've been rode hard tonight."

The grim-faced deputies nodded and left.

Mrs. Baker poured milk in a steaming cup of coffee to cool it so Mr. Byers could drink it. She handed the cup to him. "This may help."

Mr. Byers winced when the coffee touched his swollen lips, but he sipped it gratefully.

Mrs. Byers stood still, as though she were in shock. She had not yet spoken.

"We found him upriver," Sheriff Underwood said. "Those skunks heard us coming and lit out. There were five of them. The four that took him and a fifth man who was keeping a pot of tar melted over a fire. We found a sack of pillow feathers. At least we scared them off before they added feathers to the mess."

Joseph seethed in anger as he stared at his stepfather. Mr. Byers's shirt had been stripped off. His hair was completely matted in tar, and splatters of tar also covered his chest and back. The skin around the splatters was red from the heat of the tar.

Mrs. Byers suddenly seemed to shake off her

horror and spring into action. "Joseph, get me my scissors. We are going to need some liniment and hot water and towels."

"I'd better go help my deputies," the sheriff said awkwardly.

"You probably saved my life," Mr. Byers mumbled through swollen lips. "I'm grateful."

Sheriff Underwood nodded. "That's my job. Wish I had gotten there sooner." He left just as Mr. Baker returned from the kitchen with a big pan of hot water and a bar of strong soap.

Joseph brought the scissors and handed them to his mother. "What do you want me to do?" he asked.

Mrs. Byers concentrated on the scissors as she snipped away each mat of hair. She hesitated. Then she said, "Take a dull knife and start scraping the tar."

David and his parents helped Joseph, while Mrs. Byers gently washed the cuts and bruises and rubbed them with a soothing salve. Mr. Byers sat motionless while they worked. Once or twice a soft moan escaped his lips.

"Oh!" Jared, still in his nightdress, was standing by the door. His eyes were wide with surprise. "What's wrong with Papa?" he asked in a tearful voice.

"I'm all right," Mr. Byers called. "I just got into some sticky tar. Everyone is helping me get it off."

"Does it hurt?" Jared asked

Mr. Byers shook his head reassuringly. "Not a bit."

Mrs. Baker took Jared by the hand. "Thou must be hungry. Let me fix thee some food."

Just then there was a knock at the door. Everyone in the room froze—except for Jared. He ran to the door to answer it.

"Jared, no," screamed Mrs. Byers.

Jared paused, his hand still on the knob. He looked bewildered. "It's just Mr. and Mrs. Taggert."

Mrs. Byers sagged with relief. Then she collected herself and answered the door.

Mrs. Taggert handed her a covered dish. "We heard about your troubles in town," she said. She caught sight of Mr. Byers, and her hand went to her mouth.

Mr. Taggert stepped forward. "We just wanted you to know not everyone in town is against you."

"I never thought anything like this could happen in Branson Mills," said Mrs. Taggert. She was a mousy-looking woman, but anger brought a rosy glow to her cheeks. "This war is turning neighbor against neighbor. My best friend turns her face away from me if we meet on the street, because my son John has joined the Union army. Her son was John's best friend. He's joined up with the Rebels."

Jared stood next to Joseph. His thin face was drawn and pale as he listened to the grown-ups. "Why did Mama scream when I answered the door?" he whispered.

Joseph hesitated. "She was afraid some bad men were outside," he finally said. "But don't worry— the sheriff will get them." Joseph was quick to reassure his brother, but he was not so certain. If the men had made it home, their attack would be difficult to prove, and in spite of the Taggerts' visit he doubted that any jury from Branson Mills would convict the attackers.

Mr. Byers had hardly spoken since the sheriff

had rescued him. With the help of the Bakers they had managed to get off the worst of the tar, although there were still splotches across his back and chest. In some places the hot tar had burned the skin underneath, and blisters had formed. It was clear Joseph's stepfather was in pain, but he maintained his dignity as he stood and gravely thanked the Taggerts. After they had gone, however, he sat back down, suddenly looking older.

"I am sorry that I have brought this on my family," he said heavily, "that I have made my wife fear to open her door. I was so sure that I was right and that nothing should stand in the way of spreading my message."

"The sin is on those who attacked thee," said Mr. Baker. "Thy message was true."

For the first time Joseph saw doubt on his stepfather's face. "Even the president has not come out against slavery. I don't know of one person I've convinced for all my talk."

"Have you changed your mind about slavery?" Joseph cried.

Mr. Byers shook his head. "No. Nor have I

changed it about the states' having no right to secede. But the time for words has passed. My decision to join the army was the right one," he said. "Slavery will never be ended until the South is crushed."

THIRTEEN

Off to War

It was several weeks before Mr. Byers was recovered enough to head north. Most of the tar had been scrubbed off by then, although a few stubborn traces remained. His burns had healed, and a new stubble of hair grew over the spots on his head where his wife had shaved off the mats of tar.

A few days before his stepfather left, Joseph walked to town with him. Not much had changed since the night of the fire. Some of the burned debris had been hauled out of town, and a few of the shops left standing had been newly whitewashed. But nothing had been rebuilt, and there were still glaring holes where the burned shops had stood. In spite of the cleanup the town looked empty and dismal.

They walked quickly past the rubble of the factory. Mrs. Byers had given them a list for the general store. The garden had yielded a few fresh greens, but it was too early for most of the vegetables.

The last time Joseph had been to the store, it had been packed with goods. From floor to ceiling the shelves had been jammed with small tools, household items, cloth, and foodstuffs. Now the shelves were nearly bare.

"We were hoping to trade off some of the money from Joseph's carving for food," Mr. Byers said.

Mr. Johnson shook his head. "The Yankees and the Rebels both have blockades on the rivers to stop supplies from getting through. It's already getting hard to find things like sugar, salt, and coffee. I've got enough flour and some sacks of beans. I've got some coffee too, but the price has gone up to a dollar a pound."

The little store was crowded. Several people spoke to Joseph and his stepfather while they waited for Mr. Johnson to gather the things on the list. Some expressed sorrow and shame for the way Mr. Byers had been treated. For the most part, however, they were greeted with snickers and knowing looks.

Andrew suddenly pushed open the door. Ham followed behind. "I need coffee and sugar," Andrew said.

Mr. Johnson's lips tightened, but he measured out sugar and a sack of coffee beans and weighed them.

Andrew suddenly spotted Joseph. "Well, well, look who's here." He pushed the slave in front of Mr. Byers and Joseph. "These people are abolitionists, Ham. Do you know what that means?"

"No, suh," said Ham. "I surely don't."

Andrew chuckled. "These are the people who think you ought to be free. Ham and I used to play together when we were little," Andrew said, turning to Mr. Byers. "Now he's my personal servant. My family takes care of him. We feed him, give him clothes and a place to stay. Ham is very happy where he is. Tell him, Ham."

"Massa Turner's good to me," Ham said. "No need to be free."

Andrew smirked. "Oh, Mr. Byers, my father said to tell you he is so sorry to hear about your troubles," he said with exaggerated politeness.

"Thank your father for me," Mr. Byers answered calmly. "And tell him I still think that slavery is wrong."

Andrew thrust the sack of coffee at the slave to carry. Without another word he slammed out the door. Ham turned back and looked at Joseph and his stepfather. A faint smile flickered and then died as he saw Andrew watching him. "Oh, by the way," Andrew said at the door, "I saw your little washerwoman friend a few minutes ago. Don't you want to run and help her carry her baskets?"

The store was suddenly silent after Andrew left. Mr. Byers paid for their purchases quickly, and they went out into the bright sunshine.

"I hate him," Joseph muttered as they stepped outside.

Mr. Byers stopped and faced Joseph. "Hate will eat at you," he said. He tapped his chest. "It will harden your heart and cloud your thinking. In the end it will hurt you more than it will hurt them."

"Don't you hate the men who did that to you?" Joseph asked as they started for home.

"I'm trying not to," Mr. Byers said. He chuckled for the first time in weeks. "I must admit I strongly dislike them, though."

Mr. Johnson ran out the door after them. "Here," he said, handing them a small sack. "This is for that sick young'un of yours."

Mr. Byers took the sack and thanked Mr. Johnson.

"It's just an orange and some candy," said Mr. Johnson, waving away his thanks. "You can have some of that candy," he told Joseph. "But save that orange for the little one."

"Thank you, Mr. Johnson," Joseph said. He selected a peppermint-flavored stick for himself. "Jared will be mighty happy to see this."

They walked in silence a few more minutes. "I'm depending on you while I am gone," Mr. Byers said. "You are young for so much responsibility, but it can't be helped."

"I'll do my best," Joseph answered with a confidence he didn't feel.

A few days later Mr. Byers was gone. Mr. Baker

drove the family to the train station, and Mr. Byers boarded a train for Indiana. From there he would travel to Washington. "I'll feel better traveling on Yankee territory with these papers saying I'm an officer in my pocket," Mr. Byers had explained.

Joseph could not help remembering the bands playing and the excitement when they'd said goodbye to Zachary. Now Mr. Baker was the only person besides his family to see Mr. Byers off, and their mood was sad rather than jubilant.

After her husband had left, Mrs. Byers put on a cheerful face in the daytime, but at night Joseph heard sobs from her room. Jared spent a lot of time looking out his window, watching for his stepfather's return.

There was little time to grieve, however. The garden Joseph had tended all summer suddenly yielded baskets of produce. In addition to his regular chores, Joseph helped his mother. The shelves in the cellar were soon lined with barrels of potatoes, squashes and pumpkins, cabbages, dried apples, and beans.

One day David stopped by with some news. "There's been another battle. This one was in Missouri. The Confederates won again."

"I wonder if Zachary was there," Joseph said.

David shook his head. "Mrs. Iverson got a letter from her son. He mentioned seeing Zachary. Mrs. Iverson's son says they are still in Tennessee. He thinks they are going to invade Kentucky. He says the feeling is that most people will join with them and take over the state."

After David left, Joseph thought about what his friend had said. If the Confederate army did take over the state, it would no doubt make things very difficult for anyone they thought was against them. Even with Mr. Byers gone, Joseph's family might be looked upon as the enemy. If nothing else, an invading army would be looking for food. Joseph thought of the food carefully stored in the cellar.

"I have been thinking about your cave," his mother said. She looked tired, and there were dark circles under her eyes. "It might be a good idea to hide part of our food there. Sheriff Underwood stopped by today. He said there are rumors of deserters from both sides hiding in the hills."

Joseph nodded thoughtfully. "I could pretend I was going fishing and take a little bit each time."

Mrs. Byers nodded. "We'll need to leave some in the cellar or it will look suspicious."

The next day his mother helped him fill a small knapsack with a pouch of dried beans, several jars of preserves, a tin of coffee beans, and freshly dug potatoes. He took along his fishing pole and a jar of worms. A few fish would make a nice change for dinner.

Joseph avoided running into anyone as he walked to the river. People did not seem to go out these days unless it was important. He looked around carefully before he climbed down the bank. Men from the Home Guard were watching the bridge. Joseph waited until he was sure they were not looking in his direction before he pushed aside the brush and entered the cave.

Inside the first room he lit the lantern they kept by the door. He walked carefully to the cavern they had discovered back in June. He quickly emptied his pack onto a dry shelf slightly higher than his head. He stepped back and held up the lantern. Then he nodded with satisfaction. Even if people were looking, they would not be likely to see the hidden cache of food. He retraced his steps to the entrance.

The men were still there. Their backs were turned so they did not see Joseph as he stepped back out and covered the cave entrance.

He had already caught two fine, fat fish when he heard footsteps behind him. He twisted around just as Hannah put down her basket. She gave him an uncertain smile. "Hello," she said shyly. "I haven't seen you for a long time."

"I've been awfully busy," Joseph stammered. He resisted the urge to check if anyone was watching.

Hannah plopped down beside him. "Catching anything?"

Joseph showed her the fish. "I think this is enough for us. Do you want to try? I've got more worms."

Hannah took the pole and expertly baited her hook. She threw in her line, and for a few minutes they sat without speaking.

"Someone came to our house," Hannah said.

"We had gone out to pick berries. When we came back, someone had written a lot of bad stuff on our door. They went into my father's workshop and broke several chairs and tables and splashed paint everywhere."

"Oh, Hannah, I'm sorry," Joseph blurted out. "Did you tell the sheriff?"

"Pa didn't want to stir up any trouble," Hannah said. "He said we'd get the worst end of it if we did. He's thinking about moving north, at least until this is over."

Joseph waited until Hannah had caught another fish and headed home. He watched her struggle with the heavy basket and felt a pang of anger against the committee. Mr. Byers had made people angry at his speeches, but Hannah's family were hardworking, quiet people who never bothered anyone.

For the next week Joseph carried knapsacks full of food to the cave. Each time he stayed until he had caught a fish or two. On the sixth night he returned to find that Clay had come home. His brother looked older. There were dark circles under his eyes as though he hadn't slept for a long time. He didn't wrestle or rub his knuckle on Joseph's head as usual. He sat down heavily at the kitchen table and cradled the cup of coffee his mother had prepared for him.

Joseph handed his mother that day's catch of fish. "Those look good," Clay said. "I haven't had any fresh fish for a long time."

FOURTEEN

——◆——

Clay's Story

"It was terrible," Clay said as he ate. "A few lucky ones found a bed with local people. The hospital was full, so they were crowding the wounded into a school. Even so, there were so many that some had to wait for days before anyone tended them. By then most had gangrene, and there wasn't anything to do except cut off their arms or legs. The stench was awful. Clouds of flies swarmed over everything. And the moaning." Clay put his hands over his ears as though he could still hear it.

Mrs. Byers held his head against her and smoothed his hair. "You must try to put it out of your mind," she murmured. There were tears in her eyes.

Clay fell silent, but after a minute he said in a normal voice, "Do you remember that I told you before how fussy Dr. Mercer is about keeping everything clean around sick or wounded people?" When Mrs. Byers nodded, Clay went on. "Well, the other doctors made fun of him because he insisted we wash our hands between patients. He made me boil bandages too and scrub the tables after an operation. I noticed a difference. Dr. Mercer's patients did better. When I'm a doctor, I'm going to keep everything washed."

Mrs. Byers put her arms around his shoulders. "You're too young to have seen such things."

"Dr. Mercer didn't even know how bad it was going to be," Clay said. "All those boys went marching off like it was going to be some big adventure. Instead they walked right into a nightmare."

"Let's not talk about it anymore," Mrs. Byers said as she put more fried fish in front of Clay.

Joseph's brother stayed for two days before he returned to Dr. Mercer's house. "I'll be glad to get back to running errands and mixing powders," he admitted.

A few days after Clay left, Joseph was sitting on the porch with Jared playing a game of checkers when he heard the clatter of horses' hooves. To his dismay it was Andrew. Joseph walked to the street to meet him.

Andrew jumped off his horse. Still holding the reins, he grabbed the front of Joseph's shirt with his other hand. "Where are the slaves you are hiding?"

Joseph was genuinely surprised. He tried to wrench free of Andrew's grip. "I didn't even know about any slaves escaping," he protested.

Andrew's voice changed, and it sounded almost like pleading. "My father has gone to negotiate a price for our tobacco crop. He'll be back tomorrow. I have to find those slaves before then. Or at least one of them."

Joseph stared at him. "Who are they?" he asked.

Andrew hesitated for several seconds. "Last night a couple of field hands ran away. Ham went with them."

"Ham?" Joseph thought back to the day at the store. "I thought Ham loved being your slave," he couldn't resist saying.

"I don't know why he ran away," Andrew said. "He got better food and clothes than the other slaves, and he stayed in the big house."

"Maybe it was because he slept on the floor by your room," Joseph said.

Andrew's face darkened. "Our overseer is already searching. My father will never allow him to escape. He'll find Ham. And when he does, he'll have him whipped and then sell him to one of the big plantations in the South."

"What do you want me to do? I'm telling you the truth. I haven't seen him," Joseph said.

"Your stepfather knows people. That Underground Railroad everyone talks about," Andrew said.

Joseph shook his head. "My stepfather has been gone for weeks. I don't know anyone."

"I'd better not find out you were lying," Andrew said fiercely as he took back his reins.

Joseph stared after Andrew as he rode away. "If I did know, I wouldn't tell you," he said out loud to himself.

There was a rumble of thunder off in the distance. Joseph quickened his steps. He reached the porch just as a torrent of rain fell from the sky.

Joseph thought about Ham. Had he found shelter from the storm? He tried to imagine what it would be like to be on the run. How would you know whom to trust?

Joseph went to bed, but he couldn't sleep. He got up and sat by his window. The rain had stopped, and a heavy fog shrouded the house. Abe padded in from Jared's bedroom. He stood on his hind legs and put his front paws on the sill. He whined softly.

"What's the matter, boy?" Joseph said, patting him. "Don't you like the fog?"

Abe growled softly, deep in his throat.

Joseph stared out. It wasn't like Abe to act so nervous. "Mrs. Byers's hens were making a commotion, squawking noisily. Could it be a fox or a raccoon? Joseph pulled on his pants and boots and went out in the hall. His mother was just coming out of her own room. "What is it?" she asked. "Did you see something?"

"I think it's a fox," Joseph said. "I'd better go out and see."

His mother touched his arm. "What if it's not?"

Joseph stopped. "What else would it be?"

His mother nodded. "I'll go with you." She raised the chimney on the lamp that was on a small shelf in the hallway and lit the wick. Holding it high to light the way, they went downstairs.

"Wait," said Joseph's mother. "Mr. Byers left his gun." She took a small key from a hook and unlocked the gun cabinet.

Joseph waited impatiently. The noise from the chicken coop had increased. Joseph looked out the window, trying to see through the fog. Suddenly he noticed something that made him freeze with his hand still on the door. A ghostly light wavered by the alley. A dark shape, walking on two legs and much too large to be a fox, passed in front of the light.

FIFTEEN

A Night of Fear

Joseph heard a sudden shout. The light flickered and went out but not before he had seen several more men in the glow. Suddenly a shot rang out, followed by another. Only a few inches from his head, the glass in the window shattered, sending slivers tinkling to the floor.

"Get down," he shouted.

His mother was still standing by the gun cabinet, holding the gun loosely in her hand. When Joseph shouted, she crouched and blew out the lamp.

Another volley of shots burst forth, and a bullet ricocheted against the wall. Joseph crawled away from the window over to where his mother still crouched.

"Who is it?" she whispered. "Did you see?"

Joseph shook his head and then realized that his mother couldn't see him. "I don't know," he said. "I could only see shapes."

Joseph's eyes adjusted to the dark enough to see that his mother still held the gun. "They'd better not try to come in here," she said grimly.

From the top of the stairs came Jared's voice. "What's happening? Are there soldiers attacking us?"

"Stay there," Mrs. Byers and Joseph shouted at the same time.

"Sit at the top of the stairs, Jared," Joseph said, keeping his voice calm. "You'll be safe there. We don't really know what's happening."

There were more shots and a shout. An upstairs window shattered, and Jared cried out, "Mama!"

Mrs. Byers, still crouching, ran to the bottom of the stairs. "Don't move, honey. I'm coming."

There was a pounding on the front door. Joseph's heart leaped into his throat. "It's Sheriff Underwood," a voice shouted. "Are you all right in there?"

"We're all right," Joseph shouted.

"Stay where you are," the sheriff called. "This will be over soon."

"What's happening?" Mrs. Byers cried. There was no answer, and they heard heavy footsteps running on the porch.

Joseph crawled across the room and followed his mother up the stairs. They huddled together, squeezed on the top steps. Mrs. Byers put the gun on the step in front of them, in easy reach. She sat in the middle, her arms around the boys. They waited while the minutes ticked away. It was silent now, the battle over, but they dared not move. Joseph leaned against his mother and closed his eyes.

Several hours went by. Joseph caught himself nodding off, but each time he jerked himself awake. Jared was asleep, half-sitting with his head in his mother's lap. The room became less dark and then bathed in a pinkish glow as the sun burned away the fog.

At last Mrs. Byers moved and stretched her cramped muscles. Jared sat up and rubbed his eyes. "Is it over?"

"I think so," Mrs. Byers answered. "You boys stay here. I'm going downstairs."

As she stood up, there was a knock at the door. "It's Sheriff Underwood," he called. "You're safe now. Can I come in?"

Mrs. Byers ran to answer the door. Joseph and Jared crowded behind her.

"Let me make you some coffee," Mrs. Byers said. While she measured out the coffee and added kindling to the big iron cookstove, Joseph got a broom and swept up the bits of broken glass. Several minutes passed.

"Some of those deserters up in the hills decided to raid the town last night," said the sheriff finally. "They had hit quite a few houses before some of the Home Guard came across them. Unfortunately," he said, eyeing the broken window, "they caught them in your chicken coop, coming out with four or five of your best hens."

"Did you get all those men?" Joseph asked.

Sheriff Underwood shook his head, as Mrs. Byers filled a cup with the freshly brewed coffee. "We're not sure, son. Killed one, got another one hurt pretty bad, and two more. Might have been some of them slipped away in that fog. It was so thick it was hard to tell what was going on."

"Were any of our men hurt?" asked Mrs. Byers.

Sheriff Underwood stirred some milk in his coffee and took a sip. "Ahh," he said. "That's good coffee. My wife tells me I'm going to have to stop drinking so much. Coffee is getting so expensive, folks are grinding up chestnuts for a substitute." Realizing he hadn't answered her question, he smiled. "My deputy Tom got a bullet in his arm. Nothing serious. Dr. Mercer's fixing him up right now." He paused. "Mr. Lippit got grazed in the head, but he'll be all right too."

"Mr. Lippit, the bookstore owner?" asked Joseph. "I didn't know he was in the Home Guard."

The sheriff shook his head. "He's not. He's going to answer some questions from me soon as he's able. Like what was he doing out so late at night. Especially when the Vengeance Committee had just paid a visit to Mrs. Fosey. She just found out her husband was killed. Here she is a grieving widow and someone painted *traitor* in red paint all over the outside of her house."

The sheriff stood up and swallowed the last of

his coffee. "I'll send someone over to help board up those windows. With your husband's business burned down, you'd have to send away for glass. That might take awhile." He handed the empty cup to Joseph's mother. "If there is very much of this kind of fighting, there might be some people in town who wish they hadn't driven your husband out of business."

Mrs. Byers smiled grimly. "I can't afford new glass."

"Winter's coming," the sheriff said. "Might be that having boarded-up windows is warmer anyway."

Joseph followed the sheriff out the door. "You didn't hear anything about any escaped slaves with all this, did you?" he asked.

Sheriff Underwood shook his head. "I haven't heard."

Joseph quickly told him about his conversation with Andrew.

"I'll keep an eye out for Ham," the sheriff said. "Andrew's right about one thing. I wouldn't want to be in Ham's shoes if Mr. Turner gets ahold of him. He's got a reputation for being pretty harsh. And that overseer of his is even worse. Well, let's hope the boy is far away from here by now."

After the sheriff left, Joseph swept up the broken glass from the floor in his parents' bedroom. As he promised, the sheriff sent a deputy with boards and nails, and the windows were quickly covered. Mrs. Byers pulled the curtains, hiding the covered windows. It made the rooms darker, but there were other windows to let in light.

"I'm going to see if Mrs. Fosey needs help," Joseph said after breakfast. When he arrived, he saw that several men were already hard at work covering up the letters with fresh white paint. Some were still visible, and Joseph stared at them before they were covered by the last brush of paint. There was something odd about them. Then he realized what it was. The letters were all slanted backward as if they had been written by a left-handed person. Mr. Healey was left-handed. He had said so the day he interviewed Joseph for the paper. He had to tell the sheriff.

As usual the sight of town depressed Joseph.

Little more had been done in the last few weeks to restore it to what it had been before the war. Only the people seemed changed. Before the fire, women had strolled holding parasols to shade them from the sun and wearing wide skirts that nearly blocked the sidewalks, and friendly groups had chatted outside every shop. Now the few people on the streets hurried about their business, exchanging suspicious looks. Several people stared at Joseph as he raced through town.

The sheriff's horse was missing. Joseph stopped in dismay. He looked in the door of his office. He could see the prisoners in their cells. There were two of them; they stared at him, hollow-eyed and ragged. Neither was wearing shoes. One of them wore the remains of a soldier's jacket, but it was so dirty Joseph could not tell what color it had been originally.

Tom, the deputy, was at the desk, reading a dime novel with a bright orange cover. "Sheriff took some men up in the hills to look for the rest of those deserters," he said. "Can I help you?"

"Did Mr. Lippit admit he was part of the Vengeance Committee?" Joseph asked.

Tom smiled grimly. "He said he couldn't sleep, so he took a walk. Don't worry, though. We're going to be watching him very carefully."

"I think Mr. Healey may be part of it too," Joseph said. "This morning I looked at the letters on Mrs. Fosey's house. They all slant to the left. Mr. Healey is left-handed. He told me that the day he interviewed me for the paper."

Tom nodded. "Good detective work. I'll tell the sheriff when he gets back. We'll need more proof than slanted letters. But this will give us something to think about."

The door opened just as Joseph got up to leave, and Andrew's father barged in. There was a spot of red on each of his cheeks, and his voice shook with anger. "I've got three runaways," he shouted. "Somebody in this town is helping them, and I'm going to find out who."

Joseph shut the door and stepped outside. Andrew was sitting on the sidewalk. His face looked glum.

"You didn't find him," Joseph said.

Andrew looked up, squinting in the hot sun. "A lot you care."

Without his friends, Andrew didn't seem quite so bold. Joseph sat down beside him. "Maybe he got away. He's had a day's head start."

Andrew shook his head. "You don't know my father."

"Then you'd better find him first and help him," Joseph said.

Andrew looked at him. "I wanted to make him come back home. I can't help him get away. He's a valuable piece of property. He belongs to my father."

"He's a human being who wants a chance to be free," Joseph said.

"Get away from me with that Yankee talk," Andrew said with a cold look, "before I tell my father."

SIXTEEN

A Daring Plan

The next morning Sheriff Underwood stopped by with a big ham. "My wife sent this over," he said. "She says we've got plenty."

"We can't accept this," Mrs. Byers said.

"Yes, you can. I'll be insulted if you don't. Anyway we do have plenty. My wife's father butchered a hog awhile back. We don't have any young ones, so it would take us forever to eat all that."

Mrs. Byers took the ham. "Tell Mrs. Underwood we are grateful."

Sheriff Underwood brushed off her thanks. "The real reason I stopped by is to tell you the news. I got a telegram this morning. It looks like the Confederate army is getting ready to invade Kentucky.

I have a feeling lots of people will be pretty upset over that. Even folks who are for the Rebels."

Mrs. Byers's eyes widened. "Will they come here, do you think?"

Sheriff Underwood shook his head. "I doubt they'll come this far north. I think they're hoping the people will join with them to take over the state. I've heard talk about them trying to set up another state government."

"Did Mr. Turner find his slaves?" Joseph asked.

"Not yet. He is roaring around, making a lot of noise, but no one seems to know anything. He's got him some dogs now, and he's planning to search the other side of the river. At least that will get him out of my hair for a while."

Joseph started. Hannah's house was on the other side of the river. What if the escaped slaves had decided to go there for help? Would Hannah's family have felt obligated to help them in spite of the risk? And what about Mr. Turner? Even if the slaves were not there, he might make trouble for the Douglasses.

Mrs. Byers was watching him. She gave him a

warning look when he opened his mouth to speak. Joseph gave a slight nod to show he understood. If Ham was there, the sheriff would have to obey the law and return the slave to his owner, and he would also have to arrest Mr. Douglass.

"I'm going to Hannah's house and warn them," he said after the sheriff left.

"It's not our business," said Mrs. Byers.

Joseph shook his head. "Hannah's my friend. I've denied it just so people would like me. But Mr. Byers is right. Sometimes you have to stand up for what you believe no matter what happens."

Mrs. Byers slowly nodded. "All right. But be careful. Just warn them and come home."

Joseph took off, running for the river. Suddenly he stopped. Hannah was smart. She would know that her house would be searched. Maybe the slaves were already far from Branson Mills. But if they had made it to her house, he knew exactly where she would have taken them.

He climbed down the bank and headed for the cave. Hannah was sitting on a rock not far from the cave. She jumped up when she saw Joseph.

"You have to trust me," Joseph said. "Are you hiding the escaped slaves in the cave?"

He could see the conflict on her face as she hesitated. "Only Ham," she said slowly. "The other two got away. But Ham twisted his ankle and couldn't keep up. I didn't know what to do with him."

"It's too late to help him escape," Joseph said, "especially if he's hurt." He thought quickly. "Maybe he could pretend that the others forced him to go with them and he just got away."

Hannah frowned. "He won't go back."

"He'll get caught if he doesn't. Can't you make him understand that?"

Hannah frowned. "Someone is sure to see him before he gets to the Turners'. No one will believe him anyway. They wouldn't believe us, either."

"Andrew," Joseph said. "He was willing to help before."

"Do you trust him?" Hannah asked.

"We don't have any other choice," Joseph said grimly.

Joseph raced toward town. What if he couldn't find Andrew? Maybe he was with his father, searching the other side of the river. His thoughts tumbled over one another as he ran. He reached the main street of town and looked around desperately. At first he didn't see him. Then, just as he was turning away in despair, he saw Andrew's horse tied to the rail by the general store. Andrew was sitting on the edge of the wooden sidewalk staring at him.

"I need to talk to you," Joseph said.

Andrew looked puzzled. "This'd better be important," he growled.

Joseph took a breath. "Did you mean what you said about wanting to help Ham?"

Andrew jumped up and grabbed the front of Joseph's shirt. "So you do know where he is!"

Joseph stared at Andrew and didn't speak. After a minute Andrew released him and stepped back. Joseph thought he saw new respect in his eyes. "I meant it," said Andrew, "but it's too late now."

"Maybe not," Joseph said, explaining his idea.

When he was finished, Andrew nodded. "It might work."

"Promise me you won't make Ham suffer for this," Joseph said.

Andrew gave him a steady look. "If what you say

is true, just coming back is punishment enough from Ham's point of view."

Andrew mounted his horse and reached a hand for Joseph to scramble up behind him. He then set his horse in a smart trot. As they neared the river-bank, Joseph's heart sank. He was going to have to share the secret of the cave with Andrew. He sighed. It couldn't be helped. It wasn't the same now anyway, he told himself. He thought back to when he had first discovered the cave and the happy days he'd spent with Zachary and David. It seemed a long time ago.

They tied the horse at the top of the bank, and Andrew followed him into the cave. Hannah and Ham were waiting in the first cavern. Andrew's eyes widened as he looked around the cozy space. Ham sat waiting on a rock ledge. He looked frightened.

Without speaking Andrew bent down and picked up several lengths of rope coiled neatly by the entrance. Hannah looked alarmed, but Andrew threw the pieces to Ham. "Tie these on your wrists and ankles. You'd better rub them back and forth so it looks like you've been trying to get loose."

Ham bit his lip as Hannah and Joseph rubbed the rope until they drew blood.

"How could you have been so stupid?" Andrew shouted. "Do you know what my father would have done to you when he caught you?"

"I know," Ham answered.

Andrew just shook his head.

Joseph peeked out, watching until the two Home Guards were looking the other way. Then, supporting Ham between them, they managed to get him up the bank and settled on the back of Andrew's horse.

"Do you think your father will believe the story?" Hannah asked.

"I'll make him believe it," Andrew said. "Who would ever suspect that a slave would run back to his master?"

SEVENTEEN

Trouble for Hannah

"I'd better get home," Hannah said after Andrew and Ham had left.

"I almost forgot," Joseph said. "I was coming to warn your family." He sniffed the air suddenly. "Do you smell smoke?"

Hannah looked across the river. Her eyes widened with fear. "I have to go home," she said.

"Wait," Joseph yelled as she ran for the small rowboat she used to cross the river. He caught up to her and grabbed her arm. "You could be heading into danger."

"My mother and father are there," Hannah said, wresting free. "And my little brother and sister. I have to help them."

155
★

"I'll go with you," Joseph said. He climbed in the boat and grabbed the oars.

"Hurry," Hannah urged.

Joseph nodded grimly, pulling the oars with all his strength. Instead of heading to the small dock where Hannah usually tied her boat, he rowed to a small woods a few yards down the river. By now they were close enough to hear shouting and the crackle of flames. They jumped ashore and quickly tied the boat to a small tree.

"Come on," Hannah said. Crouching low, she led the way through the trees.

Joseph grabbed her arm before she burst into the clearing. "Be careful. You can help your family a lot more if you're not caught too," he whispered.

Hannah made a visible effort to calm herself and nodded. Together they slipped through the woods and crouched at the edge of the clearing, hidden by brush. Hannah's breath caught in her throat, and a small moan escaped her lips. Joseph grabbed her arm for support.

The little cottage was engulfed in flames. Mrs. Douglass was sobbing, her arms protectively around the two youngest children. But it was Mr. Douglass who was in the greatest danger. His arms were stretched high and tied to a wide, straight branch of a tree. Four men in black hoods were there. One of them stood behind Mr. Douglass with a menacing whip in his hands. Mr. Turner stood a few feet away, watching. "Where are my slaves?" he asked.

"I don't know," Mr. Douglass answered.

At the same moment, the man with the whip flicked his arm, and the whip lashed across Mr. Douglass's bare back.

Forgetting all caution, Joseph jumped out of his hiding place. "Stop," he screamed. "You are making a mistake. Mr. Douglass didn't have anything to do with the slaves escaping."

The man with the whip lowered his arm. As he did, Joseph caught sight of a small crescent-shaped scar on the back of his hand.

"Stay out of this, boy," said Mr. Turner. "It doesn't concern you."

Angry now, Joseph whirled to face Mr. Turner. "Yes, it does concern me," Joseph said. He was aware that Hannah had crept out of her hiding place and was standing near her mother. "Mr. Healey isn't even part of our town. You've let him come here and terrorize people. Mr. Lippit?" Joseph said, staring at the other men, trying to identify the bookstore owner. "Mr. Healey came here writing all that stuff about hate in his paper and organizing this group to attack anyone who didn't think like himself. People like Mrs. Fosey. You know her, don't you? Every time someone is sick Mrs. Fosey bakes muffins and brings them. She's probably done it for some of you. But you let Mr. Healey write terrible things on Mrs. Fosey's house right after her husband died."

The men shifted uncomfortably, looking at one another.

"They are traitors to the South," Mr. Healey shouted.

"I think Mrs. Fosey loves Kentucky as much as you," Joseph said. "More. You aren't even from here."

"I don't care about any of that," Mr. Turner said. "I came here to find my missing slaves."

Hannah spoke for the first time. "We found Ham. Andrew is taking him home. The others tied him up and left him in a cave so he couldn't stop them from heading north to see if they could join the Union army. No one helped them at all."

The clearing was quiet except for the roar of flames. The roof suddenly fell with a shower of sparks and a billow of black smoke. One of the hooded men turned and walked over to his waiting horse, and the others followed one by one.

"Stop," Mr. Healey shouted. "This changes nothing."

One of the men paused. "This changes everything. It's too bad it took a child to bring us to our senses."

Mr. Turner reached into a saddlebag and pulled out a knife. Mrs. Douglass gasped in fear, but Mr. Turner reached up and quickly cut through the ropes holding Mr. Douglass. Without another word he mounted his horse and followed the other men.

EIGHTEEN

Afterward

The next morning Sheriff Underwood came at breakfast. Joseph was trying to eat, unable to shake off the nightmarish images from the night before.

"Sit down, Sheriff," Mrs. Byers said, pouring him a cup of the precious coffee.

"Those poor people," Mrs. Byers said. "Joseph told me what happened. He's going to take them some quilts and vegetables from the garden as soon as he's done eating."

Sheriff Underwood shook his head. "No need now. They're gone."

Joseph jumped up, nearly knocking over his chair. "Gone? Where?"

"Headed north. They left last night. I sent Tom

after them to make sure they got across the river without trouble. Didn't want anyone thinking they were escaping slaves."

"They didn't even say good-bye," Joseph said, sinking back down in his chair.

"Oh, yes," the sheriff said. "They did stop and see the Bakers before they left. Said they were thinking about heading out to Oregon to make a new life for themselves. Guess they figure that's about as far away from here as you can get." He reached in his pocket. "I almost forget. They left something for you." He handed Joseph a piece of paper folded in half. Slowly Joseph unfolded it.

> I'll remember Branson Mills
> And the times both good and bad.
> I'll remember you, Joseph,
> And the friendship we had.

Joseph smiled. When he and his friends had begun to fix up the cave, they had found playful notes signaling that another shared their secret. That other was Hannah.

Sheriff Underwood headed for the door. "And I almost forgot the major reason I came," he said. "I thought you might like to know the news. The Confederate army from Tennessee did cross over into Kentucky yesterday. This morning a Union general named Grant marched into the northern part of our state near Paducah. The state legislature has asked Washington for help. President Lincoln told them they had to choose. The governor didn't make any secret that he'd like the state to go with the South. So the legislature forced him to resign. Looks as if Kentucky is going to be part of the Union."

Mrs. Byers sank down in her chair. "I can't believe it. What are all the people who are for the South going to do?"

The sheriff shrugged. "Some of them have already packed up and left. One of them was Mr. Healey. He didn't even stop to pick up his clothes. I imagine he knew I was about to arrest him. He told some of the men he was joining the Confederate army. Mr. Lippit said Healey was the one who set Mr. Byers's factory on fire. Mr. Lippit named a couple of other people, so I think we've seen the last of the Vengeance Committee."

"Thank heavens for that," Mrs. Byers said.

After the sheriff left, Joseph sat for a long time looking at the note. Mrs. Byers sat down beside him. "Do you think I will ever see Hannah again?" he asked.

Mrs. Byers shook her head. "Oregon is a long way from here."

"I wish I'd been a better friend," Joseph said.

"You made up for it in the end when you stood up to all those men," Mrs. Byers said. "That was very brave."

"It would have been braver to have been a good friend all along."

"It's hard to be brave all the time," Mrs. Byers said with a thin smile. "I suppose if I were brave, I would ignore those women at church and attend this Sunday."

Joseph stood up and offered his arm to his mother. "Let's practice," he said. "We shall just march in with our heads up high." Putting on haughty faces, they strolled around the room.

"That's the first time I've seen you smile in weeks," Joseph told his mother.

Just then Jared came to the door. "Why is everyone so happy?" he asked.

Mrs. Byers grabbed his arm so he could join in the parade. Around and around the room they danced until they collapsed on the floor, laughing.

Mrs. Byers smiled. "What would Mr. Byers think if he could see us now?" she said.

Joseph winked at Jared. "I think Papa would be proud," he said.

More about
Joseph's Choice—1861

Kentucky was situated between the southern states and those that supported the Union. It was bordered by several important rivers: the Ohio, Tennessee, and Cumberland, all of which could transport men and supplies. Kentucky's position was so important that President Lincoln is reported to have said, "I hope God is on our side but I must have Kentucky."

For the first few months of the war Kentucky was able to remain neutral. Although it did finally choose to stay with the Union, its citizens were almost equally divided in their sympathies. Kentucky escaped most of the terrible fighting, but the people paid a heavy price. Perhaps more than any other state, Kentucky's division caused friends and even families to bear arms against one another. The bitterness of these divided loyalties lasted for generations.

During the war, locomotives were tipped over, and bridges and railroads were often destroyed to slow the delivery of supplies and prevent the movement of troops. The Union worked on the bridge problem, and by the end of the war they had perfected a prefabricated bridge that could be constructed in twenty-four hours. Locomotives were hard to remove from the tracks and therefore did more lasting damage.

The Civil War was the first time that trains were used to move goods and men. It was at least part of the reason the Union lost the first big battle of the war at Bull Run. The Confederates were able to move in fresh troops to fight Union soldiers already weary from a long march to the battlefield.

The North and South often had different names for battles. The first big battle was known as Bull Run in the North and First Manassas in the South.

It was not until shortly after the war that doctors

accepted the idea of germs and the importance of keeping wounds clean. As a result, thousands of soldiers died of infection from their wounds. Doctors moved from patient to patient without washing. Often dirty bandages were taken off dead soldiers and used again.

The use of the telegraph and the invention of photography kept civilians at home informed about the war. Photographers and journalists followed the troops and reported back. Because the enemy often cut telegraph lines, journalists learned to send all the important information in the first paragraph, a style that is still used in today's newspapers.

At the beginning of the war most soldiers were paid about thirteen dollars a month. Soldiers on both sides had to scrounge for food. Both armies did provide biscuits or crackers called hardtack. These were so hard the soldiers called them teeth dullers. The crackers often became infested with weevils that hatched their larvae in them; some soldiers called them worm castles. Because scurvy—a disease caused by not eating fruits and vegetables—

was common, the Union army later issued squares of dried vegetables. Soldiers called them hay.

Soldiers had to prepare their own food. In addition to all their other equipment, they had to carry cooking and eating untensils. Southern soldiers often brought their slaves to camp to cook and clean.

Here are some interesting fun facts:

Were you as surprised as Joseph that the lizard found in the cave had no eyes? Creatures that have lived for generations in the dark evolve with no eyes, although some still have a dark spot of useless flap where the eyes once were.

Did you notice that when Joseph's mother leaves the room, she has to push her skirts through the door? In the 1860s fashionable ladies wore huge hoops under their skirts, making them so wide it was hard for them to pass though a door.